SWALLOW'S DANCE

SWALLOW'S DANCE

DANCE

WENDY ORR

pajamapress

www.pajamapress.ca   info@pajamapress.ca

 Canada Council Conseil des arts   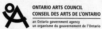 ONTARIO ARTS COUNCIL   Canadä
for the Arts   du Canada   CONSEIL DES ARTS DE L'ONTARIO
                                                an Ontario government agency
                                                un organisme du gouvernement de l'Ontario

The publisher gratefully acknowledges the support of the Canada Council for the Arts
and the Ontario Arts Council for its publishing program. We acknowledge the financial
support of the Government of Canada through the Canada Book Fund (CBF) for our
publishing activities.

Library and Archives Canada Cataloguing in Publication

Orr, Wendy, 1953-, author
Swallow's dance / Wendy Orr.

ISBN 978-1-77278-062-8 (hardcover)

   I. Title.

PS8579.R77S93 2018   jC813'.54   C2018-902143-8

Publisher Cataloging-in-Publication Data (U.S.)

Names: Orr, Wendy, 1953-, author.
Title: Swallow's Dance / Wendy Orr.
Description: Toronto, Ontario Canada : Pajama Press, 2018. | Summary: "A priestess by
   birth on the Bronze Age island that is now Santorini, Leira finds her coming-of-age
   training cut short when an earthquake destroys her town and leaves her powerful
   mother disabled. Warned by an oracle that worse is yet to come, the family flees to
   Crete but finds no sanctuary. A tsunami sends the island into anarchy and Leira must
   hide her noble status and learn new kinds of strength to help what remains of her
   family to survive."— Provided by publisher.
Identifiers: ISBN 978-1-77278-062-8 (hardcover)
Subjects: LCSH: Bronze age -- Greece – Juvenile fiction. | Tsunamis -- Juvenile fiction. |
   Fantasy fiction. | BISAC: JUVENILE FICTION / Historical / Ancient Civilizations. |
   JUVENILE FICTION / Action & Adventure / Survival Stories.
Classification: LCC PZ7.O77Sw |DDC [F] – dc23

Cover and text: based on original design by Design by Committee
Cover and interior illustration: Josh Durham
Map illustration: Sarfaraaz Alladin, www.sarfaraaz.com

Manufactured by Friesens
Printed in Canada

Pajama Press Inc.
181 Carlaw Ave. Suite 251 Toronto, Ontario Canada, M4M 2S1

Distributed in Canada by UTP Distribution
5201 Dufferin Street Toronto, Ontario Canada, M3H 5T8

Distributed in the U.S. by Ingram Publisher Services
1 Ingram Blvd. La Vergne, TN 37086, US

For Claudia and Olive,
who bring joy to my life

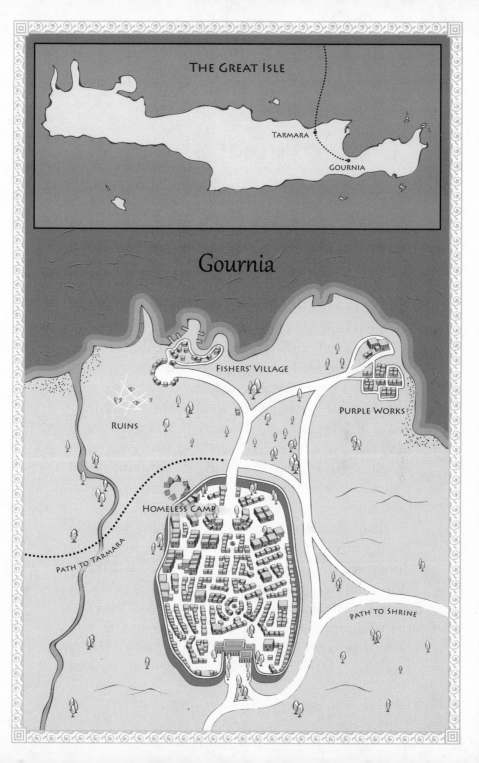

AUTHOR'S NOTE

Around four thousand years ago, a great Bronze Age civilization grew up around the Mediterranean island of Crete. To its north was the island of Thera, now know as Santorini.

In 1625 BCE, Thera experienced one of the greatest volcanic eruptions in human history.

The island and its prosperous harbor town, which had traded luxury goods and raw materials as far as Egypt, Cyprus, the mainland of Greece, and Minoan Crete, were completely covered by yards of lava, ash, and pumice. It was a dead and forgotten place for several centuries, and even when people began to resettle, the original inhabitants and civilization were forgotten except in strange myths of Atlantis.

Three thousand years later, archeologists began to dig through the layers of ash and eventually discovered a sophisticated town of two- and three-storey houses, painted with elaborate frescoes. It seemed that catastrophic earthquakes had heralded the final eruption: the people fled; they had time to bury their dead and remove their valuables. There are many different theories on where they went and what happened in that time; for this story I've chosen what makes sense to me.

The more I studied this civilization, the more intrigued I became by one of the frescoes—a painting of girls in ceremonial dress picking crocus on a mountain. The girls are so individual that I became convinced they were portraits of real people. There's no doubt that they would have been from the most privileged class—and yet, if they survived to flee the volcano, they would have had to start their lives again as refugees. This is how I imagined the story of one of the girls in that fresco—the snub-nosed saffron gatherer.

SONG FOR
KORA THE MAIDEN

Kora, Kora, born of the goddess,
your fleet foot wounded in wars of the gods;
when swallows fly you across the dark sea
your mother, weeping, brings death to our land.

Kora, Kora, your maidens call you,
your promise is woven in dance and song
let swallows fly you home in the springtime
bringing joy to our hearts and life to the land.

1

Nunu says that when the goddess belches, it means change is coming.

This is the greatest belch I've ever heard. We're halfway up Crocus Mountain, on the ridge where the grassy slope turns to rock; six excited girls and their mothers or aunts or grandmothers, warm now from the hour's walk, though our bare feet are cold. As the dawn sky streaks pink and yellow over the sea, the earthmother's body trembles like a wave. It's still quivering when the belch erupts from her mouth. The stench steams up from the deep waters of the bay like the burp of a man sick from eating three-day-old fish.

But because it's the goddess, no one coughs or waves the stink away. We all stand straight, left hands holding baskets and right hands on hearts, until the ground is still.

We'd danced our way here, toes tingling in the autumn chill; skipped singing through the awakening streets and on the road up the hills. It's the first morning of our journey to becoming women. In a year we'll be weighed down with the Learning of the Swallow Clan—the songs, dances, and rites that care for our island—but this morning the goddess demanded nothing but joy.

The mothers danced too: Mama and Pellie's mama right up to the hills, and Alia's grandmother hardly at all, but even she smiled and swayed as if her mind was dancing. And they all sang. I never knew women so old could still be girls when they wanted.

Pellie, friend of my heart,
    born the same spring—
    playing, talking, growing together
    all the days since then
    until she started her bleeding
    six moons ago, in the spring of this year.
    Preparing to enter her Learning,
    wearing her flounced skirt and shift,
    leaving behind the tunic
    and shaved head of childhood—
    and me with it.
One by one, the girls of my clan
    started their bleeding—
    even Alia, youngest of all—
    till I wondered if I'd be left
    a child forever
    and alone.
"Be patient," said Pellie—
    as if she were wise and old

with barely time to speak to a child—
for she was deep in the mysteries
of becoming a woman
and we could no longer share
our thoughts and laughter.
More alone
than when Ibi married,
leaving this house for his new wife's family,
or when Glaucus sailed to Great Island
to be ambassador there for our small land—
because my brothers are so old,
nearly twenty summers,
we have shared much,
but never our thoughts.
More alone even
than when Dada sails each spring
with his ships full of goods
to trade in the farthest points of the world—
because Dada always comes back.
And though Pellie hadn't left
I didn't know if she'd return
to be my heart-friend again
if I didn't start my bleeding
before this night's full moon.
Then my despairing Mama
when the moon was nothing but a crescent line
sacrificed a goat to Great Mother,
collecting its blood in a bowl,
telling Cook Maid to prepare a pudding
with that red blood

and singing loudly to the goddess
till I'd eaten it all,
my belly full to cramping—
and the next day, my bleeding came.
At last, I entered the Lady's House,
to live in silence with the goddess;
my head shaved one last time—
one curl at the front and tail at the back
the promise that my hair will grow
thick and curly as my cousin's has.
Released from silence as my bleeding ended,
washed and dressed in my fine new shift
I stood before the shrine
for the Lady to wrap me
in my wide flounced skirt
so all the world could know
I'm a Learner in the Swallow Clan.
Now Pellie and I
are on the journey together,
sister-friends again.

The earth is still moving.

Is the shaking all over the island, or just here on the mountain, a sign to her maidens?

Mama drops her hand from her heart. "Gather well," she says, not mentioning the belch or the shaking, so we don't either. We spread out across the ridge, searching for the goddess's sign that life will renew again now the autumn rains have come. The morning is dawning bright and sunny, and we need to gather the crocuses before the dew dries.

I find one quickly, pale purple petals blooming against the rocks, yellow stamens and long orange stigmas waving.

"Pick from above," Mama tells me. "Don't let them turn upside down." She shows me with her fingers, and I pluck my first crocus, laying it gently in my basket so that not one grain of the precious saffron will be lost. Now I know why we had to weave the bottoms of our baskets so tightly. I wove ten before I got it right, and wondered why I couldn't just take one from the kitchen, but it makes sense now I'm here: my offering in the basket I wove.

I spy another flower further up the hill, and climb toward it, my bare toes monkey-sure on the rocks, bracelets and anklets jingling. Mama watches closely, but I must be doing it properly because her eyes close in the autumn sun, welcome after days of rain. I climb further. Another crocus and another, higher up the hill and around, ignoring rocks under my feet and prickles scratching my ankles, till my basket is full. When I straighten I can't see anyone else, not Mama or the other girls or their mothers. The town and its harbor are below; but now I can see the bay again, the deep blue water in the crescent of land, and the rocky islet in the center where the goddess's breath hovers.

A sudden twittering fills the air. A cloud of swallows is passing overhead, leaving us for winter. I call them to stay, because they'll take the goddess's daughter with them and there'll be no warmth till they return—I'm not ready to be stuck inside weaving for long wet days.

But I'll be part of the swallow dance tonight!

It's almost worth seeing them go. I stand and watch them out of sight, hand on heart.

I try not to look at the little dots of boats on the bay. I wonder if the boys are out there, on their own quests. We all know that fishing is part of their initiation, just as they know crocuses are part of ours, but the details are secret, and we mustn't talk to each other during our Learnings.

But that doesn't mean we can't think about them, or that Pellie and I don't wonder what they have to do, and how they're going, and most of all, who we'll choose when the time comes for us to marry — whether it will be one of the boys we know, or someone from outside.

Mama says the Learning will tell us, and we'll know when the time is right.

I hope so. Because I can't even imagine it.

I find two more crocuses and balance them on top of the purple mound in my basket.

"Thank you, Great Mother," I say. Joy floods through me like sunshine. Ever since I started the tasks that would lead to my Learning, if I do one tiny thing wrong, Nunu tells me how lucky I am to be born into this family, because my skills would never be good enough to be craft-folk. But the truth is that the Swallow Clan's work is what matters. We offer the rites the gods demand, and the other clans serve us so we can. That's the only way our home and its people can thrive, because we're not simply priests and rulers — we're the bridge between the land and the gods. And today the goddess is pleased with me.

Then she hiccups again. Her shaking throws me to the ground; I land on my hands and knees, dirtying the beautiful skirt it's taken me so long to weave. My right hand is scraped and bleeding; pain shoots up my left arm. Worst of all, as my wrist bends backwards, I let go of my basket. It bounces down the rocks, scattering the precious flowers—purple petals, yellow stamens and sacred orange stigmas—across the hill.

In the silence
      as the goddess stills,
      girls are screaming,
      mothers calling
      and I am sliding
      eyes tear-blurring
      scrambling to each flower
      to brush off the dirt
      and lay it carefully in my basket
      as if it had never fallen.
Hearing Mama's voice,
      "Leira, Leira!"
      and calling back,
      racing around the rock
      into her arms.
But the hug is quick
      now she knows I'm safe
      and she calls out to know who's hurt
      and if all are here.

Rastia's mother
　　has a twisted ankle;
　　Alia's basket is bent
　　because she sat on it hard
　　and Pellie's bitten her lip,
　　trickling blood down her chin.
　　There are bruises and grazes,
　　skirts dirtied and even torn,
　　but nothing worse
　　and as Pellie and I stare and whisper—
　　I show my red wrist
　　but don't mention
　　dropping the basket—
　　Mama shouts
　　that we must return now
　　and present what we have
　　at the temple.
Mama has a loud voice
　　so people generally
　　do what she says—
　　and we all need to see
　　what's happened in the town.

"Pellie and I can run ahead," I suggest.

"You're carrying offerings to the goddess," Mama snaps. "We'll take them to the temple in the proper procession."

Her voice is sharp with fear, the same fear I can feel in my belly—because my belly doesn't care that the earth is the goddess's body; it just knows that the ground shouldn't move like the sea.

But we're gathering her crocus! She would never harm us on this day!

This is the ninety-ninth year since the earthmother's shaking destroyed the old town. Now we have the most beautiful city on earth. Dada talks about the places he visits on the ship: cities that have been there since before memory. Even when he tells us eye-flashing, hand-waving stories of giant pyramids and other wonders, he admits that parts of these towns are old, dirty and crumbling. They're not painted in new styles every second generation, like the shrines of our temple and homes.

"Our mothers were painted together," I heard Mama snap at Pellie's mother one day last spring, when Pellie had started her bleeding and I hadn't. "We can't break the tradition!"

". . . but if Leira hasn't started . . ."

Mama gave a huff that I didn't know she'd use to her cousin.

"She was named for my mother . . . of course she'll be there."

When I was little, I thought Nunu was my grandmother. Saying so was the only time Mama's ever smacked me: "My mother was Swallow Clan, not a slave!"

I haven't got it wrong again.

Whatever this painting is, I'm guessing it's in part of the temple that I haven't been admitted to yet—and that I'll see it soon. Because Leira, my grandmother's name and mine, is the name of the goddess's autumn flower, the saffron crocus we've picked today.

The goddess shakes again, a long, trembling sigh.

If the temple falls, I'll never see what Mama was so upset about.

It won't fall. The town's buildings are strong and new, built to shake and keep standing when the goddess belches.

"Sing!" Mama commands, and we gather closer together, the women leading us on the path down the hill, along the ridge where we can see the ocean dark and blue on both sides of the island. We're singing for the goddess, but she helps us in return, chasing away fear with our songs.

We pass the wishing tree, an olive planted at the spring by the goddess herself with a hole in its ancient trunk just big enough for a girl to slide through, leaving her wish in the tree like a snake leaves its skin.

No time for wishing today—Mama leads us straight past, barely slowing to salute the sacred tree. Now we have to walk fast and try not to breathe in as we sing, because the wind is gusting up from the south, bringing the stink from the purple works.

"Aren't you glad we didn't have to make our own purple dye?" Pellie whispers.

I can see Mama listening. I don't answer, just crinkle my nose in disgust so that Pellie nearly laughs, and her own mother turns sharply.

But we'd never have to make our own purple. Mama says the Learning teaches us how things work in the world: like making the baskets, we need to understand dyeing so that everything we weave, or have our servants weave, will be as beautiful as it can be. We collected madder roots and weld plants, mashed and boiled them to make our own red and yellow dyes for our skirts, but the few drops of purple came in a tiny flask, like one for perfume, with the smell gone.

The goddess loves purple in every shade, from the pale mauve-blue of her crocus, to the blood-darkness of the richest murex dye. But the only thing we need to know about the dye is that we're the favored few with the right to wear it.

I sing a little louder in praise.

When I was small
    I followed Nunu wherever she went
    and on once-a-moon family days
    we visited her brother and his wife.
    There Nunu's nieces—
    and their husbands and children—
    are always in the workshop,
    carting red soil and white,
    mixing and pounding it into clay.
    They round balls in the palms of their hands,
    thumbs in the middle to pinch out a pot,
    smoothing and fining the edges
    with nimble fingers.
    They roll tubes long as snakes
    to coil upwards into jars
    taller than my head,
    taller even than the grown-up nephews.

The sister-in-law who rules it all
        throwing a lump on the wheel,
        spinning it round,
        the pot growing tall between her hands —
        and all of them singing,
        coaxing the clay into a pot —
        or plate or vase,
        a drinking cup or sacred jug —
        whatever the gods call up
        through the potter's hand and mind.
Or so it seemed
        to small Leira,
        watching potters' fingers
        form effortless magic
        while my own stumbled
        over a small lump —
        my snakes bloated
        my pots lopsided
        no matter if I held my breath or sang,
        my work always
        slapped back into clay
        to be remixed and used again,
        never good enough for the kiln.
        In this workshop
        it doesn't matter who you are,
        only the worth of your pot.
Till I was ten
        or perhaps eleven
        and pinched out a bowl,
        fine and even;

good enough, said the old ones
　　to be baked and saved.
Mama's smile when she saw it
　　was knowing and wise
　　but the bowl was placed in a basket
　　and never used—
　　the best I'd done
　　was not good enough.
I sulked to Nunu
　　"I wish I'd been born to a family like yours!"
　　And Nunu laughed
　　till she spluttered and choked,
　　"A family like mine,
　　who sold me to your grandmother
　　to pay their debts!
　　It was that or go down
　　to purple slavery,
　　never admitted to town again—
　　I saved them from that, at least,
　　till my young brother grew lucky
　　and married into the clay.
　　But even in this workshop,
　　do you see them living in a house like yours?
　　They make the pots
　　but your family trades them—
　　it's to the Swallow Clan the profit goes.
So never wish
　　for what you don't know—
　　because if you do
　　the gods may hear."

Of course, when I said that I wished I'd been born into a family like Nunu's, I meant the family her brother had married into: craft-folk who are as free to travel the world as my captain father. Sometimes I look at the life my mother leads, ruling our home and slaves, second only to the Lady in leading our clan, and I want to break free as a fledgling trying its wings.

But I hadn't known that people from other clans could become purple slaves. The ones who've been born into it are used to stinking like rotten shellfish and not being allowed into town, but it would have been terrible for Nunu. She was lucky that my grandmother bought her—though I only said that once.

"May you never need luck like that," she'd answered, with a look that made me shiver.

I wonder if purple works girls have their own kind of Learning when they start their bleeding—and quickly make the sign against evil. The goddess is grumpy enough—I don't want to make her any angrier by thinking about that disgusting clan on a sacred day.

The path widens and I link arms with Pellie.

The hills turn to fields; the slopes aren't as steep and the grass is dotted with sheep as well as goats. The flocks are a restless, bleating mass; goatherds are shouting and dogs barking. Their panic bleeds into us; my heart beats faster and I think Pellie's does too. By the time the town appears, I'm trembling so hard that I'm not sure if it's me or the earth. For a moment I imagine the buildings tumbled, the bright rocks, red, black, and brown, strewn like counters in a game . . .

The town is whole. From here we can see it laid out like a mosaic, the farms leading to the small houses and workshops, then the flat roofs and windowed top floors of the great buildings in the center, the shadowed triangle space between our house and Pellie's and the road leading down to the temple and the harbor.

I'm concentrating so hard I forget to sing, but now the chorus swells:

As the goddess wills,
so all will be well.
She gives us life,
we offer her ours
and all will be well.

I join in, and know it's true.

As we reach the farms, people are outside their houses, looking nearly as lost as their sheep. Two houses have broken walls, and the farmers are so busy staring at them or moving furniture into an animal shed that they forget to salute us. *Don't they know we're carrying the great mother's flowers?* We sing louder till they put down what they're carrying and stand with their hands on their hearts.

The path becomes a road that splits into a web of narrow streets, covered with the dust and rock shaken from house walls. A path has been swept down the middle of the street from the Lady's House to the temple, small piles of brick shards, pebbles and dust on either side.

This is not how our procession should be, but Pellie and I walk down it, arms still linked, trying not to step on the gravel.

I hope Nunu is watching from the window as we pass our house.

You're not a child now! I remind myself, and don't turn to check.

At the door of the temple, Pellie and I squeeze hands—we never need words for what's in our hearts—and go to our mothers. Two by two, we step inside, Mama and me first, then Pellie and her mother, and the others after.

And two by two, we sigh with relief: there's no hint of dust or disturbance here. *Of course the goddess would never harm her own shrine!* The smooth vestibule floor is soothing on our scratched feet; the stone benches are cool on our bottoms, even through our heavy skirts. We sit and study the paintings: the goddess's daughter Kora, her wounded foot dripping its life blood onto a crocus; one of her maidens offering her a necklace of golden beads, and the youngest maiden, veiled in the fishnet shawl of the swallow dance.

No one's told us what happens in the Learning. Even this morning I didn't know we were going to pick crocus until Nunu put out my ceremonial shift and flounced skirt. The shift is red, finely woven with a pattern of stars and dark bands on the front edges and sleeves. It's longer than my girlhood tunics, going nearly to my ankles. The sides and front are open so I can walk free, though when my skirt is wrapped around me, nothing can be seen that shouldn't.

Nunu dropped the shift over my head, helped me lace it up to cover my breasts, then pulled it smooth and even to wrap the skirt around my waist, tying the long sash with a bow at the back.

The shift is much finer than anything I could weave. The skirt took long enough—last winter I felt as if I never left the loom, Mama was so worried about my finishing it before I started my bleeding. When she put it in a chest without saying a word, I thought she'd noticed where I'd pulled too hard and a line had puckered. I wonder what happens to girls who don't ever weave their skirts straight, or make their baskets tight, or find crocus flowers in the mountains? What if they never finish their Learning?

But Mama smiled this morning when I came out in my finery, and Nunu wiped her eyes when she thought I wasn't looking. Mama gave me new gold hoops for my ears and Dada gave me an anklet set with blue lapis lazuli and bright rock crystals that shine in the sun.

I look down quickly, glad to see it's still there, not pulled off by a prickly branch when the earthmother shook. The bracelets on my puffy left wrist aren't as loose as they were this morning, but at least I didn't lose them.

Two maids place basins of water on the floor, and we wash our faces, hands, and feet free of dust. Mama smooths my short fuzz of hair.

"Come, Leira," says the young priestess, appearing in the doorway so suddenly I jump. She's three years older than me; her name is Kora now that she's the Lady's assistant as well as her daughter, though I remember when she was Gellia and lived next door.

My heart is thumping as I pick up my basket. It thumps harder when I follow her up the staircase, between the painted scenes of Crocus Mountain. I'm climbing steadily closer to the earthmother's mysteries, and I don't know if I'm ready.

At first all I can see is the Lady on her tall ceremonial chair, her eyes dark with kohl and her necklaces of golden dragonflies glowing. Then I realize that every wall is painted with the story of the crocus. Behind the Lady, the goddess is seated on her painted throne, a monkey offering her a crocus and a winged griffin standing guard behind. But the strangest of all is realizing that the girl pouring crocuses into a pannier is little Alia, while on the other side of the window, Pellie, red curls and all, balances a full basket on her shoulder. And on the next wall, talking to Kora who used to be Gellia, is a gatherer with a shaved head and a turned-up nose: me.

It's as if the great mother has been with us on the mountain all day, watching and painting instead of belching and shaking.

I don't belch, but I do tremble.

"Oh!" is all I say, before Kora shakes her head and I close my mouth again. No wonder the mothers were arguing, because Rastia, Tullie, and Chella were picking today too, and they haven't been painted. Every one of them has longer hair and a straighter nose than me and would look better on the wall—because even Pellie could never pretend that my nose is straight. If I were a clay statue, the potter would be sent back to reshape it.

Now that ridiculous nose is there for every maiden and woman to see, until after I'm dead and gone.

Better than not being there at all!

I'm especially glad I'm there instead of Rastia, because her nose may be perfect but her spirit is mean. The only thing she's said to me since her first stay in the Lady's House was, "You'll understand if you ever start bleeding . . . it's too bad you won't do your Learning with Pellie and me."

Suddenly I don't care about my snub nose, because I'm the one who's on the wall with Pellie.

Mama's eyes flick
    and she almost smiles,
    as the Lady watches me
    blush red as my shift.
    But I remember to salute—
    hand on heart, eyes down—
"Praise the mother of all,
    mistress of animals,
    goddess of saffron,"
    I say, and the Lady nods.

Her warmth glows like sunshine at noon
and when Kora holds out a pannier
I pour in the flowers from my small basket—
a tiny offering in the great.
Kora points to a chair and a stool
so Mama and I sit
while Pellie's mother
and Pellie come in.
I see my friend staring,
hear the same, "Oh!",
and she too turns red
as a sunburned fisher—
and adds her flowers to mine.

I watch the other girls as they take in the paintings—
Rastia bites her lip, but Chella smiles in surprise at
recognizing us. I don't know if I'd have smiled if it
had been her instead of me.

The Lady begins to sing the story of the crocus,
which is also the story of the earthmother's daughter,
who dies when the swallows leave and is reborn when
they fly back in spring. It's very long—but finally we
are chanting, "Kora, Kora, your maidens call you!" and
following Kora who used to be Gellia down the stairs.

I can't help a little sideways glance at my portrait
as we leave.

But I'm also starting to think about dinner, because
it's a long time since breakfast. Maybe I could sneak a
couple of figs or honey cakes from the kitchen as soon
as I get home. I'll ask Nunu to draw me a bath too,

because I'm tired as well as hungry and I can't wait to tell her about the painting.

But Kora leads us to the back of the temple and pours the precious flowers out onto a table. The room floods with scent.

"Your mamas will do one first," she says, and we watch, our empty baskets at our feet, as each mother picks up a crocus.

Mama pulls the petals back to where the three red threads become one, pinches the pistil out from the yellow stamens around it, and places it in a dish on the center of the table. The petals are dropped into my empty basket.

Pellie's mother sniffs with annoyance. I'd been concentrating too hard to realize that it was a race, but of course it is. And of course Mama would win.

"Speed is good," says Rastia's mother, "but an offering to the goddess requires perfection."

Mama points to a second, plainer dish. "Exactly. Any damaged ones can be used for trade, but only the perfect will go to the goddess."

She's won again, because she was perfect as well as fast, and by agreeing she's turned the reproof into praise.

I will never be as smart as my mother.

"Goddess guide your fingers, Learners," says Kora, and I reach for my first flower. It's fiddlier than it looks, and takes long moments.

I catch Pellie's eye. I wonder if being on the painting means that we should be good at this, and if it's a bad omen that I'm not.

The pile of flowers looks much bigger on the table than it had in Kora's pannier. It doesn't seem to be getting any smaller.

The mothers are eagle-eyed, watching each other's daughters to see that we don't miss a stigma or waste a grain of the precious saffron. Pellie sneezes, blowing petals across the table. Rastia laughs and Pellie looks as if she might burst into tears.

"Breath of the goddess," says Kora, and Rastia tries to change her laugh into a sneeze too.

But now a yellow stamen is in the pot of perfect red threads.

"Who did this?" Rastia's mother hisses. "Are we Egyptians, to cheat the goddess?"

My mother's eyes narrow. Everyone knows that Dada's grandfather was Egyptian.

Kora snatches the yellow thread and drops it into the nearest basket. "No harm is done when quickly mended."

It's the only thing that's quick. By the time Chella lays the last three stamens in the pot, our fingers are stained red, our stomachs are rumbling and we look as tired as servants.

But we still need to follow Kora and the pot into another undecorated room, hot as a midsummer day, with a fresh crack in the wall that we pretend not to notice. Kora spreads the threads on a fine mesh over a brazier, sings a quick prayer, and leads us out again.

"Farewell, Learners," she says.

We're free.

Mama takes my hand as we cross to our home. "My almost-woman child," she says, and kisses my forehead.

Nunu greets us at the front door, guarding us from the uproar in the kitchen. She's nearly in tears as she tells Mama that the maid Tiny was carrying a tray of honey cakes up the stairs when the house started shaking. She was thrown to the bottom, bruising her leg and bumping her head on the hard stone steps; the tray broke and the honey cakes were smashed. She kept falling over every time she stood up and Nunu finally sent her to bed. Worse, Cook Maid dropped the bucket of snails and by the time they'd got Tiny settled the snails had disappeared into corners—they've only just got half of them back again.

"And upstairs—" Nunu adds, as if she might as well get all the bad news over with at once.

"Not the shrine?" Mama interrupts.

"No, not that," Nunu says, and Mama breathes a sigh of relief. "But the swallow vase that belonged to your grandmother fell off the windowsill and smashed in the street. I cut my foot when I went out to see." She lifts her skirt to show the cut foot, but Mama is already rushing up the stairs to check the rooms herself.

The shrine room looks bright and clean, the red stone floor shining as if no dust dared to make its way in here—no, it's damp under my feet; it's just been washed. Only the swallow vase is gone from its window niche, disappeared as surely as the swallows I saw fleeing this morning. There are a few small cracks in the frieze around the top of the walls—a warrior has lost his spear and one of the ships has a gap in its sail. It looks unlucky and I hope the painter can fix it soon. But the shrine table in the corner is clean, waiting for offerings, and the boys on the walls are still walking toward it, carrying their fish.

Which reminds me. "Nunu, we've been to the temple and I'm—"

"Leira!" Mama snaps, quickly making the sign against the evil eye. Nunu is making it too, as if she knows what I was going to say. They both look shocked, and now I am too. *How could I be so stupid?* Pointing my fingers, hoping it's not too late, wondering what ill luck I could have brought against myself.

But how did Nunu know?

The painter! She's visited so often since my bleeding, coming upstairs to chat to Mama while we were weaving. All the while she was observing me, storing me in a secret place so she could put me on the wall. My parents must have shown her the earrings and anklets before they gave them to me.

"The jewelry is the Saffron Maiden's, first made for your grandmother's grandmother," says Mama. "I've kept it safe for you since my mother died."

I don't remember my grandmother's face or anything she said, but I remember knowing that I was special to her.

"But who has that Saffron Maiden been since then?"

"The goddess and her attendants exist without us," says Mama. "They don't age or die with the faces borrowed for their paintings."

I'm still thinking about this when Dada comes in. He puts his hands on either side of my face, studying it. "My almost-woman child," he says, just as Mama did, and kisses my forehead.

The sea smell is strong on him, which is strange because the ships are stored in the shipsheds for the winter, their sails and rigging being mended and spliced.

"Has the captain been paddling at the beach like a small boy?" I tease.

Everyone freezes. I don't need Mama's warning glare to stop talking; my fingers flash again: *I'm sorry, earthmother, forgive me, god of the sea, I didn't mean to ask about sacred secrets. But even though I guessed that the Learning boys were on those boats in the bay, how could I know that Dada would be guiding them?*

I should have. What other man of the Swallow Clan is a ship's captain, the master of our trading fleet? When the room we're in now is the sea god's shrine?

What happens to a Saffron Maiden who offends the gods twice on her first day? Three times if you count dropping my basket.

"Leira's bath is ready," Nunu calls, and I escape up the stairs.

The bath is hot and scented, strewn with petals of summer-dried flowers and orange threads of saffron. The water turns gold and so do I. I'm truly a Saffron Maiden. I absorb the knowing with every fiber of my body, and the more golden my skin becomes, the more I feel it with pride instead of fear. I see the line of Saffron Maidens stretching back through time to my great-great-grandmother, and know it goes on back past her, to before our town was built. One day I will have daughters, and a daughter and a granddaughter and great-granddaughters who will follow on till the end of time.

Nunu brings me honey cakes and cheese to eat in the bath, and ale to drink, and I know that she wants me to go on soaking up the saffron for as long as possible. Finally she holds out a towel, and I step out of the tub so she can pat me dry. The yellow stain doesn't rub off; I study my outstretched golden arms as Nunu dresses me, and they are beautiful.

My embroidered red shift has been shaken clean; the three layers of my woven skirt have been brushed and the small tear from a prickle bush mended. Even my jewelry has been rubbed to a new glow. Nunu smooths olive oil onto my fuzzy head, and brushes my forelock and pony tail into loose curls. She tugs hard at the tangles the way she always does, making me yelp, and then snaps at me to hold my head still as if I were a child.

But when she tells me to go to my mother, it looks as if there are tears in her eyes too.

Mama is in her room, freshly clean and made up, though the make-up pots are still open and she's holding the fine brush in her hand. I sit on a stool and she works on me like the painter worked on the wall. Bright pink lips and nails, and rouge-red cheeks like hers, but instead of kohl, she smudges a saffron paste on my eyelids and the tops of my ears, till they are as yellow as my stained fingers.

A shiver like the earthmother's trembling runs through me—the face in the mirror belongs to the Saffron Maiden on the wall, and I don't know if I'm still me underneath.

Mama opens the chest under the niche where the house goddess sits, and takes out the tiny bowl I made last month. Each of the Learners made one, but I was the only one who'd played with clay before—and Nunu's brother's family are the best potters in the land. They make the fine pots for our clan and the temple, and the swallow pots that Dada trades around the world.

It was Nunu's sister-in-law herself, younger than Nunu but twice as cranky, who taught the Learners. She pretended that she'd never seen me before, though of course Pellie knew the truth. And suddenly I understood Mama's knowing smile about the little pot I took home when I was a child—maybe it wasn't just that it wasn't good enough to be used. Maybe she didn't want anyone to know I'd already played at one of the crafts of the Learning. Better to let everyone think that even a girl who's late to bleed can be gifted at something.

Now, my shift laced to just below my breasts, my skirt swinging, my wrists and ankles jingling, I take my little bowl and follow my mother into Triangle Plaza.

The street is empty. Women wave from the windows, but servants, children, men and boys are forbidden to see us until the goddess has received our gifts. And yet, if Dada spent the day with the Learning boys, surely they'll be going to their part of the temple too.

What if we see them? What if I bump into a boy and have to marry him at the end of my Learning?

I don't even want to think about it!

But if any boys are in the temple, they're safely hidden in their own section. Only Kora waits for us in the entrance.

In the hot, heavy-scented drying room, she portions out the dried saffron threads into our tiny bowls. We climb the Crocus Mountain stairs again, bowls held reverently in our two hands, mothers following with our baskets of petals.

The Lady, waiting on her throne, beckons for us to tip our saffron into the urn on her lap. With a moistened, crimson finger, she draws a sacred three-in-one pistil on our cheeks.

Kora hands her a jug of honeyed wine, and the Lady pours it into our empty bowls, draining the last of it into two cups for herself and Kora. "Drink, crocus-learners," she says, "for not a grain of the goddess's saffron must be wasted."

She drains hers at a gulp, throws her cup to smash on the altar stone, and watches us with a strange half-smile. I gulp mine down in the way Mama has always taught me not to, and smash my bowl.

I was so proud of that little pot. I thought it would stay in our house forever, to be treasured like my great-grandmother's swallow vase—though that's smashed now, too. Wine and emotion are spinning in my head, and then I understand. Making pots is not for the Swallow Clan. I see my childhood dream smashing with the bowl, but there's no time to feel sad because Kora has picked up a flute, and the Lady is dancing.

"Come!" she calls, and the six of us join hands to circle her. Our hearts are thumping; our legs are awkward, afraid of stumbling or kicking the Lady by mistake. Then the mothers begin to ululate, shrilling an exalting *lu-lu-lu* over Kora's high, wild music, and we circle faster and faster, finally breaking free to whirl and spin as the Lady does, our ponytails flying like her long black curls. The mothers toss the flowers from our baskets; mauve-tinged petals flutter like butterflies before being trampled underfoot. The room fills with the sweet crocus scent, flooding my senses like the honeyed wine; the other girls are a blur and so are the mothers—all I can see is the Lady, still dancing while one by one we drop to the floor around her. I can hardly tell if she's twirling or the room, except that her golden dragonfly necklaces are flying as if they've come to life.

Maybe they have, I think. *Maybe this is the magic.*

But she stops, finally—just comes to a halt, still smiling, not dropping sick and dizzy like the rest of us. She sits on her tall throne, barely panting. Her left foot is bleeding from a pottery shard, like the earthmother's daughter before the swallows take her. Mine is too. It doesn't hurt; I wonder if it's a sign.

"Goddess keep you, my crocus-learners," says the Lady. "My almost-women."

I think that means the night is over, but it's not. We drink another cup of wine, and then the Lady and our mothers sing:

Dance for the blooming crocus,
born of autumn rain,
dance for our dying Kora
crying in her pain,
dance for the flying swallows
till they bring her back again.

As they sing, our mothers drape us in the wide fishnet shawls of the swallow dance—*how could I forget?*—then Kora takes my hand—*me, the newest Learner*—to follow the Lady down the stairs and out to the street, with the other girls and mothers following. The waiting people sing with us, holding torches high as we dance through the town, our shawls opening and closing like wings of the swallows we're calling to bring the earthmother's daughter home next spring.

2

Weaving in the upstairs room—
   Nunu, Mama and me—
   companionable in the unexpected sun
   of this shortest day,
   and the anticipation
   of tonight's feast;
   our looms strung with wool for coverings
   for a bed that will be mine
   when I am a woman.
"Ha!" says Nunu, hands and shuttle flying,
   "She's wondering if she'll ever
   find a husband to bring home."
"Shush!" says Mama.
   "Tonight's the last
   Midwinter joy of her childhood—
   let her enjoy being a girl
   while she can."
My face burns—
   it's not even true that I'm still a child

but sometimes
I'm not ready to be a woman
and want my Learning to last forever—
though it's true I was dreaming
of my daughter one day
offering her saffron
and seeing me
on the temple wall.
Nunu would say I'm offending the goddess
even to think it
but Nunu doesn't always know
what I'm thinking.
I'm still wishing I could find
something clever to say
when a loom weight swings,
hitting my hand so hard
I squeak an ouch
and drop my shuttle—
while from downstairs
comes the crash of a pot
hitting the floor.
Mama and Nunu stop their weaving
and Mama rises.
"I'll go," I say,
happy to hide my burning face
in the solitude of stairs.
But I haven't reached the landing
when the house shakes
like a dog wet from the sea.
A moment follows—
shivering silence.

I turn to see
my loom weights swinging,
tok-tokking,
hitting and spinning—
then Mama is screaming,
"Get out! Away from the house, far as you can!"
And I obey, good girl that I am—
two stairs at a time
with my skirt held high,
reaching the bottom
when the house shakes again
not a dog now
but a rabbit in the dog's mouth
neck snapping,
shaken to death.
Then, like the dead rabbit
loosed from the jaws—
tossed one last time—
Mama flies
from the landing,
her head touching a step
halfway along
and tumbling the rest of the way
with no more sound than the dead rabbit
except for the thump of her head
on each step—
and though the journey
lasts a lifetime
I can't move or breathe
till she lands crumpled
at my feet.

Now I'm screaming,
    crouched at her side,
    screaming for Dada,
    for Nunu,
    or anyone to help
    because Mama doesn't move
    or speak
    and her face is all blood
    like the rabbit,
    skinned.
But only Nunu calls back—
    because Dada is at the shipsheds;
    the maids have fled
    as Mama told them
    and the great beam above the door,
    forgetting its job of holding the wall,
    has crashed in,
    bringing the wall with it
    in mounds of brick,
    painted fresco and dust—
    so we can't get out
    and no one else can get in.
Nunu calls again
    though I don't know where from
    or what she's saying
    because the house is groaning,
    the earth rumbling
    and everywhere
    people are screaming
    and walls are crashing—

and I am alone
with my maybe-dead Mama
and Nunu trapped at the top
of the broken stairs.
The stone step
where Mama rests her head
is snapped in half
like a branch over a knee
because the walls on each side
have moved in their places,
so most of each wall
is on the steps.
I can't see round the bend—
but can guess Nunu won't be here soon.
The earth's rumbling
    grows to a roar
    and now the house,
    is shaking again,
    trying to throw itself
    onto Mama and me.
The kitchen's great table is the only shelter
    but in the middle of the room,
    so far from the doorway—
    how could I drag poor Mama
    across the stone floor—
    so I run to the table
    as if fleeing a wolf,
    shove it across till it hits the wall—
    I never knew
    I could be so strong.

"Sorry, Mama," I say,
     tugging her through the entrance
     to crouch beside her
     under this new roof.

The shaking lasts for hours, days, a lifetime. The ground floor windows are small and grilled; they've disappeared completely now, but some light and then rain come in from a new gap in a wall. There's enough light to know when the dark comes.

I don't know if it's here for evening or forever.

I've been lying with my head against Mama's chest, trying to tell myself that the movement I feel is not just the goddess still shaking the house, but my mother's breath. I'm terrified that it's not true. With my face right there, I can smell her blood above the choking mist of grit and dust. Blood and the sour stink of piss, and as the floor gets colder I realize I've wet myself. I don't know when. I don't even care, and I'm not even shocked that I don't care.

A groan and another hot flood—and it's not from me. I didn't think I could ever feel so happy: Mama's alive.

I scream again for Nunu. Nunu will know what to do.

If she answers I can't hear. The goddess is still rumbling and I hate her with a blind red rage—and I'm not shocked at that either. Then I'm begging her to save Mama, promising whatever sacrifice she wants and the only one I can think of is my painting in the temple. *Take that*, I plead, *I offer it to you and all that it means, the painter can paint another maiden, but no one can make another Mama.*

The goddess doesn't care. She shudders again, dumping ceiling onto my table roof, and I'm shaking too, choking in the dust of what used to be my home. My eyes are streaming, though I don't know if that's dust or fear, because this is not how the world should be.

There are no more screams or shouts from the street. Nunu still doesn't answer. I don't know if she's dead or trapped behind rubble on the stairs. All I can hear is the grumbling of the house and the deeper rumbling of the earthmother.

She's no mother, to destroy like this!

I'm alone. As alone as anyone could be: the only one left alive, with my dying Mama.

Why didn't you finish the sacrifice and take me too? Though I don't scream it out loud, even now. The goddess has shown what her rage can do, and I don't know if I can face what she wants of me.

I also don't know how all this can race through my head while I'm still coughing, screaming, and weeping, my body trembling as much as the house.

Then my face, pressed against Mama's chest, feels a quiver. Another muffled moan escapes her lips. And finally, I understand.

The only one who can help Mama is me.

Which is almost more terrifying than being alone with her death.

So, as the shaking stops, I crawl out from under the table. Clearing the way to the outside door will take too long; I need to clean Mama off now and give her something to drink. The storage pots of food, wine and oil are stored under a bench—I can't see it in the darkness, but it's only a few paces away. All I have to do is creep along beside the wall and I'll find it.

But the floor is a pile of sharp clay shards; my palms are bleeding by the time I crawl out from the shelter of our table. My knees are too, stabbed right through the thick wool of my long winter tunic.

My sandals are by the door, lost in darkness and rubble, but there's no choice. I slide myself upright, waiting for the terrible unknown thing that will hit me, jab me, cut me. Nothing does, so I edge along, my feet tentative, feeling their way, till my right foot hits the bottom of the cupboard. Closer, and I'm touching the side; it seems to be intact, though covered by a layer of debris. The pots and ewers that should have been standing on top are part of that wreckage, their contents scattered and lost, but underneath are the niches holding the storage pots.

Bracing myself against the wall, I start shoving debris off the bench. There's wetness and stickiness, and I'm imagining even more blood and horror—is someone trapped between benchtop and rubble? My skin crawls at the thought of touching a dead maid. And how would I ever move them to get what I want?

Ouch!

A sudden sharp jab, a splinter in the side of my hand, and I'm sucking away the pain before I can think. But it's not blood I'm tasting, it's gritty, sticky sweetness — the remains of something for our solstice feast. I suck my fingers clean before tracing them gingerly across the benchtop. They find the holes for the niches; I lean closer and reach in.

Three of the big pots are broken, but there are smaller pots inside — some of them are whole, and so are all the baskets of dried foods. No point in looking for water; the giant pithos was at the door for easy refilling of jugs, and the jugs would have been on this benchtop or the table — I'm probably standing on one now. What I have is olive oil, wine, honey and goat milk. The milk is delivered for me fresh every morning, because Mama believes women need it to grow their own breasts, to feed the babies that will come after marriage. My throat is so dry and choking I drink it straight from the jug, three great gulps before I even think of sharing.

The goddess shakes again, punishing me for my greed. I feel so wicked I'd spit it out if I could. But instead of crushing me, she tumbles out a chunk of wall between kitchen and storeroom. There's no window in that inside room, but a dim light comes in from somewhere — and wherever that is, I'm grateful.

I pick my way back with a jug in each hand, dip my finger into the honey and put it to Mama's mouth. "Sacred food of the gods, feed my mother and let her wake!"

Her lips quiver, her tongue comes out to lick the honey, but she doesn't wake.

What do I do, what do I do, what do I do?

If she were a baby, she'd need changing, but the blood on her face is more frightening, so that's what I do first. One of the baskets holds a loosely woven cloth to protect food from insects. I pour olive oil onto it, and start gently wiping the blood from her forehead. At first I'm so tentative that I barely touch her; the cloth is covered with blood, but it doesn't look as if any has gone from her face. I pour on more oil and try again.

Most of the blood has come from a big cut just under the hairline, though her face is scratched and bruised all over. Her nose, that strong beautiful nose, is crooked; when I wash around her mouth her tongue comes out again, with a broken tooth on it. I take it out and put it by a table leg so we don't lose it.

By the time I'm ready to wash her lower half, it's stopped seeming strange and wrong. It's something I have to do, like some of the odder tasks to prepare for the Learning, and until I've finished I don't have to worry about what to do next.

The dim daylight fades.

In the darkness, there is no time. I don't know how long we've been here. Long enough that I have to sidle out of our table shelter again to pee in the corner; Mama, I think, has peed again since I cleaned her. There is nothing soft to lie her on, nothing dry; all I can do is smooth olive oil down her legs as I would a baby.

I will die here,
    shrivelled like a snail in summer
    in the shell of this house
    not maiden or mother or crone
    not even a memory
    if there is no one left to remember.
    Maybe Mama is lucky:
    not yet dead, but feeling nothing.
Then Mama groans,
    so I know she can feel;
    a lion fierceness roars through me
    because she is not Mama now
    but my own babe,
    and I, blind in the darkness,
    walk my fingers to the wall
    for more precious sheltered pots;
    dip my finger into honey again
    and when her tongue takes it,
    drizzle in drops of pure sweet wine—
    in hope that it will lull her pain.
"Drink, Mama," I say,
    "Drink and be well."
    And I have the same:
    honey on my tongue
    to sweeten the wine,
    then curl up by my mother
    and sleep.

A crash jolts me awake, my heart pounding. *The house is falling on us!*

But the house isn't shaking. The sound is someone upstairs shoving things across the floor.

"Nunu!"

No answer, just another crash. Nunu's not dead! She's trapped upstairs as Mama and I are trapped down here.

Scrambling out from under the table to the vestibule, I hobble to the stairs. The last time I saw them, before the roof blocked the light from the window, each step was broken in the middle and covered with chunks of wall.

Another crash. Still no answer when I shout.

Even my hands are blind in this blackness; I kneel on the bottom step, sweep my forearm across the next one to clear it, and crawl up to it. I feel unbalanced, because steps should be flat, and these slope down from a peak in the middle. The only thing that's even is how much my knees hurt, because I've only knocked enough rubble off that I can get up there. There are still lots of sharp pieces left to dig into me.

With each step there's more wreckage, and the chunks of masonry are bigger. One big piece bounces past me and tumbles to the bottom, just like Mama did. Mama who is lying helpless, just through the doorway from the bottom of the stairs.

What if it's hit her and I've killed her!

I slide down, bringing more brokenness with me, landing on the big chunk that's crashed at the bottom.

Of course it didn't bounce through the doorway and onto Mama!

How could I know that on a day when the world has changed?

I can't go back up without checking her again. My ear on her chest tells me that she's still breathing, her heart still beating. I whisper my lips over her face, guided by her breath, and meet no chunks of wall, but a taste of blood in my mouth.

I can't do this.

But I can't sit here and wait to die, or wait for Nunu to get through, which might be the same thing.

"I'll be back, Mama," I tell her. "Don't move!" Even though I've been begging her to do that since she landed here, that lifetime ago.

I creep back up the stairs, shoving and kicking the debris behind me as I climb. The blackness is still complete, and the sharp-edged shards still make me squeak and bleed, but I don't care anymore. I've tried too hard to wait and die now.

The stairs go on forever. It feels as if I've climbed far enough to be on the roof when I touch a wall in front of me—and I realize I've only reached the first bend.

No matter how hard I try to picture the stairs as they used to be, when they were smooth and straight and the staircase was lined with paintings, I have no idea how many steps there are. All I can do is creep around the bend and find the first stair. My head is spinning, and I think I might have slept for a moment—it's hard to tell in this blackness, but I hear myself calling Nunu for a cup of water, as if I've forgotten where I am and why I'm thirsty.

Nunu shouts back.

I can't quite hear the words, but whatever they are, they're better than water, better than wine, and I'm wide awake again. I scramble up the ruined stairs to the landing.

3

I know it's the landing because when I run my hands along the walls, they come to an end where there should be an opening—I should be stepping straight into the day room, and finding Nunu. Instead there's another wall.

I bang my fists on it, and it shifts a bit.

"Nunu!"

"Leira!" Her voice comes from just on the other side of this new wall. "Have you brought help? Is your Dada here?"

I've been counting on Nunu to help me, not need help!

"Just me."

"But your mama—where is she?"

There's panic in her voice—Nunu, who pulls fishhooks from fingers without a blink; who caught my brother Ibi by the heels as he fell from a window, before I was born. Nunu, who's afraid of nothing, is afraid. I can't tell her about Mama, not now.

"Nunu, what's blocking the stairs?"

"The ceiling. The pillar's collapsed . . . there's nothing left."

She's going mad. The day room is so big that it has a central pillar to hold up the roof. It's huge and strong, like the tree it was carved from. It can't just collapse.

"You shouldn't be up here—it's not safe. Go back to your mama."

She sounds exhausted. Nunu, I realize, is crying. Crying because she thinks she's alone, and that I'm free to leave the house, to find my parents and safety. And none of those things are true.

"Move back!" I say, and standing with one foot on the top step and one on the step below, I throw my whole weight at the blocking wall.

It creaks, but doesn't move. I try it again, again and again, and just when I think I can't try it one more time, it shifts and crashes to the floor. I fall through onto a pile of rubble: the pillar, roof tiles, bricks and wall plaster. My eyes are stinging and blinking, because the dawn light is streaming in where the roof used to be.

It's a miracle that Nunu wasn't crushed. Part of the roof and second floor are scattered over the day room; the wall to the shrine room is down, and the servants' stairs have completely disappeared under piles of wall. But the big windows out to Triangle Plaza are still there, and that's almost worse. Because it's not just our home that's in ruins, it's the whole town. The streets are heaped with rubble; Pellie's house is open to the world with the whole front wall missing. Further out, smaller houses and streets have completely disappeared—the town is nothing but a field of dusty rocks.

Yet the real fields, the hills and pastures, are still green and whole. It seems wrong. They should be torn apart and weeping too.

I see all this—think all this—in the time it takes me to turn my head and see Nunu. Looking as old as her own grandmother, she scrambles over to throw her arms around me. I've never realized before how much taller I am than her. It's like hugging a bony little bird.

"Where's your mama?" she asks again, and this time I have to tell the truth. She looks so fragile that I think it will break her, but instead it turns her back into Nunu.

"We've got to get back to her," she says, turning to reach for a bed covering that she must have pulled out earlier; it's spread across another piece of wall, as if to dry. "It rained in the night," she explains, and starts down the stairs.

It's easier now that there's light. Not much of it reaches under the table in the kitchen, but enough that Nunu can see my sleeping mother and her wounded face.

"What can we do?" she whispers.

That's not what she was supposed to say. Nunu is supposed to know what to do; that's her job. She always knows, even when it's something that Mama needs to decide, Nunu mutters a word or lifts an eyebrow so we all know that she could have done it better.

"More honey and wine," I tell her. "She'll take that on her tongue." Because with the dim light from the stairwell trickling in, I know what I need to do.

The front door and the window beside it are blocked by a huge beam; I can't move it, but surely I can shove the door open the way I did upstairs. I squeeze my legs under the beam and push with my feet till my stomach cramps and sweat pours down my face. The door doesn't budge.

I have to find another way.

Leaving Nunu weeping as she drizzles honey onto Mama's tongue, I creep cautiously back up the stairs. A chunk of masonry rolls from the top, crashing against the front door beam and bouncing to the kitchen doorway. Nunu shrieks with the shock of it.

"Goddess leaping! Are you trying to kill us?"

She sounds cross enough that I know they weren't hurt. I keep on going.

I was downstairs longer than I realized; the sun is halfway up now. The brightness makes the shock worse all over again: this is not my home, this pile of brokenness open to the sky.

The world outside the window isn't mine either. It's like one of the strange ruined cities in the far-off places Dada visits. And the longer I stare, the more I understand that I can't wait for anyone to rescue us.

I have to see what's blocking our door.

So I drop to my belly on the shard-sharp-floor, staring down to Triangle Plaza, wiggling out on the windowsill one painful handbreadth and another—*if the earthmother shakes me out of here I'll be dead for sure!*—until I can see the mound of bricks piled up against our wall, blocking the door and downstairs windows.

That's Pellie's front wall! Thrown all the way from her house to ours.

Where is Pellie?

No wonder I couldn't kick the door open.

My thoughts are still racing, not believing, when out of the corner of my eye I see movement

Men are clambering over the broken bricks into Triangle Plaza, Dada and Ibi in the lead.

The flood of relief
    blinds me,
    washes away my burdens
    till I'm so light I could float
    like a feather to their feet.
    For the men of the shipsheds are strong
    and will do what my father says.
They are all—Dada and Ibi too—
    covered with dust,
    red, black, and white
    like the stones that used to be our city;
    clothes torn—
    one has lost his cloak
    and another his loincloth—

and streaked with blood
    as if they were slaves.
But when I shriek
    they look up and I see
    they truly are my father and brother,
    who will save us.
I'm shouting that Mama is hurt
    and trapped,
    when the chief joins them
    and all turn to see the Lady's house
    as the ground shudders again
    and the side wall crumples
    becoming more garbage
    strewn across the plaza.
The men jump to safety;
    they don't scream as I do
    but their mouths and eyes
    are horrified Os.
"The Lady and her people
    are out and safe," says the chief,
    "turn to your own."
    Dada is already shoving,
    hauling, angling rocks with poles
    working with his men
    to clear our door
    though Ibi pauses to call me,
    "If Mama is hurt as you say,
    we'll need a bed to move her."
    He throws a rope, neatly coiled,
    and I catch,
    without knowing why.

Hot anger burns off relief—
    I thought they would fix things
    or tell me what to do
    because how will I find a bed
    under these walls
    and what am I to do with the rope?
I never knew anger could be good—
    but it pushes my floppy body
    away from the edge
    standing it upright to climb broken walls
    to where my sleeping room used to be.
    Across our bright and lovely day room,
    where yesterday, a lifetime ago,
    we sat at our looms
    and I worried about
    becoming a woman—
    now I step on something sharp
    and my foot drips blood like the dying Kora's—
    the shuttle snaps in two.
Even the wall
    between sleeping room and lavatory
    is gone, though the toilet is whole—
    the only seat in the house not broken
    so when I see it
    I can't wait any longer,
    and am grateful for the piece of outside wall
    still standing.

The sleeping room isn't quite as broken as everything
else. The clothes chest is smashed, my wall with the

swallows is gone and Nunu's sleeping mat is buried, but my bed is still there. The coverings are tumbled on the floor beside it, as if I've just got up and Nunu hasn't had a chance to tidy it yet.

I wish that was true. I wish I'd just woken and this was nothing but a demon-dream. "Shush," Nunu would say, "Open your eyes—see how the goddess has chased the demons away."

This time the demons have won.

I still don't understand how Ibi means to carry Mama on the bed, or what I'm supposed to do with the rope. And I don't know how I can push the bed across these mounds of debris and down the broken stairs.

My toes curl into the softness of the bed fleeces beneath them. I don't know what Ibi means about beds—but we can wrap Mama warmly in these and carry her to safety.

Safety? Where's that? I've seen the broken town!
Dada will know. Just do this.

I tie the bedcoverings into an awkward bundle, stumbling and falling as I try to carry it across the broken walls. My body lands soft on the bedding but my palms are bleeding again.

The men are still clearing the doorway, at the other end of the wall. I shove my bundle through a window. The fleeces and fine linen coverings slip out from my knot, landing scattered across the ground like wounded birds; the end of the rope is still in my hands.

I go back for the bed. Without the covers, it's just goathide laced tightly to a frame of wooden poles.

I suddenly realize what Ibi means. With a quick shove, I flip the bed over, thread the rope around the front strut, and drag it to the windows, hoping nothing sharp will cut the hides.

That part is almost easy. Shoving it through a window is not, and I need to lower it slowly—it won't land as soft as fleeces. I realize too late the rope needs to be at the back and now I've got it jammed partway out the window.

"Slimeface!" I swear at it. "Fishbreathed, purple-stinking billy goat!"

The bed doesn't care, but I feel stronger. I finally yank it back, pick myself up from where it's landed on me, insult it again, then stand it on end and cartwheel it over the sill and through the window.

It just fits.

I shove it the rest of the way, holding tight to the end of the rope.

"Ibi! I've got it!"

My father and brother look up, and rush toward the lowering bed.

It's getting heavier, going faster . . . If I don't let go soon it'll pull me out the window too.

They grab it just in time.

"Good," Dada calls. "Now come down before the goddess shakes again. We're nearly through to the door."

His face is gray. It's the first time I've seen my father look like an old man.

An edge of Mama's cloak is sticking out from under a pile of wall fragments. This is my only chance to get what we need, for wherever we're going. I tug it out, tearing a corner. She'll be cross when she wakes up.

"Come down now!" Dad shouts from the street.

I turn to his voice, and see my flounced skirt in the cleared space where my bed had been. Nunu must have laid it out for the solstice party. I grab it with a gasp of relief, hugging it tight as I flee. How would I have finished my Learning without it? I might never have become a woman.

4

It's like the procession of the spring festival, when the whole town carries their house goddess up to the shrine on Crocus Mountain so she can feed on the sacrifices and bring fruitfulness to the home. Except instead of goddesses carved from wood or stone, we're carrying real people of bleeding flesh and broken bone. And no one is singing.

Mama is one of the lucky ones carried on an upside-down bed, Ibi and Dada taking the front legs, two sailors taking the back. Every little while they stop and change places so the other arm takes the weight; where the path is level they lift the bed to their shoulders.

Nunu and I are carrying baskets of food: dried figs and dried fish, small flasks of honey, wine and oil. I wish I knew how to carry one on my head like a peasant. Nunu must have learned when she was young but she's too stooped now—it would topple off in front of her. The bigger baskets are strapped to our backs and we each carry another; like the men, we change arms, carry them hugged to our chests, lift them to our shoulders—anything to change the strain and lessen the pain.

In some streets all the houses are damaged; sometimes one house in the middle is standing up bravely in the midst of chaos, but Dada and the chief say we can't stop yet. The earthmother is still shaking. One tremor is strong enough to throw Nunu to the ground; I cling to the nearest wall and Dada shouts at me to move away. *But houses are safe; houses are shelter—it's hard to remember that suddenly they can kill us!*

A girl behind me drops her basket; a jug of wine breaks, dripping red over her feet, and she starts to cry.

Ibi snarls at her. Ibi's home has been destroyed; his wife and baby escaped with the rest of her family but he doesn't know where they are. Anger hovers over him like a cloud.

We walk on. I'm lucky—I found Mama's sandals in the vestibule under the big beam when the men cleared it to open the door. My feet were already so cut and grazed from the broken pottery on the floor that I couldn't have walked this far without them. And we're barely out of town yet, coming up the hill that shelters the purple cove.

The stink washes up to us. How can so much be lost and this stink remain? From the top of the hill it looks as if the buildings there aren't even damaged.

The goddess must love her sacred purple above all else, to protect its workers like this!

But even if the choice were mine, I'd never be tempted to take refuge in that stink.

It starts to drizzle. Some families stop, arranging pots and baskets around them and huddling under capes and fleeces. We trudge on: shivering, cold and sore—and I know that Mama, still and pale on her stretcher bed, will die out here in the cold rain.

Doesn't Dada realize? I hurry to catch up with him. "How far are we going? Mama . . ."

"Your mama needs more than a shelter of fleeces," he replies. "We're heading for the farms on the other side of Crocus Mountain; goddess willing, there'll still be houses standing to take in Swallow Clan. The chief and the Lady are ahead of us with their household."

"Fish," says Mama suddenly, her tongue poking out to lap at the raindrops.

Dada turns in shock, stumbling and nearly dropping his leg of the stretcher bed.

"Mama! You're awake!"

She blows a bubble and is quiet again.

"We'll catch you a fish," Dada promises.

Mama doesn't stir.

"She probably thinks she's a fish," Ibi mutters. "Swimming in the rain."

Dada glares at him. "Nunu will cook it for you just the way you like," he says.

It sounds like her song. *Maybe that's what Mama wants!* I sing it to her, the way she used to sing it to me when I was little.

If I catch you a fish,
oh my love, oh my lovely,
if I catch you a fish
will you love me too?
If I cook you a fish,
oh my love, oh my lovely,
if I cook you a fish
will you love me too?

Ibi joins in for the last two lines, but Mama doesn't stir again.

Another tremor; more people calling out to their families to stop, they're not going inside a building anywhere. Better to take their chances with falling raindrops than falling bricks. Only our kitchen maid Tiny, still carrying the ewer of ale she'd been holding when Mama shouted to get out of the house, hurries up to us. "People said you were up ahead," she gasps, breathless. "I've been trying . . ." She sees Mama, and can't say more.

But as the procession clears, I see another household is still behind us.

"Pellie!"

We rush to each other, dropping our baskets, hugging and crying, words tumbling out with our tears.

"Your house!"

"Your mama!"

"I thought she would die."

"I was so afraid!"

Her mother and my father call; we pick up our baskets and walk on, bumping sides in our closeness. Our stories become truer, more real, as we tell each other. When the front of Pellie's house collapsed, they were able to get down the servants' stairs at the back. No one was injured.

"I thought your house didn't look so bad," she says guiltily, as if she could have changed things if she'd known the truth. "I didn't know you were trapped in there."

"It was so dark, Pellie—I thought I'd never see light again!"

She kisses my cheek. "We camped in a goatfield last night—there were lots of families there, and no one had seen you. I thought . . ."

We're both crying and shivering; we're filthy, bruised, and grazed, and more frightened than we've ever been in our lives. But we're alive, and together.

"Pellie!" her mother calls. "I need you to carry the baby for a while."

I'm turning with her when Nunu stumbles. She's not going to be able to walk much farther if I don't help her. So now Pellie is acting as a nursemaid, and I'm supporting mine.

But these few minutes of walking with my friend have let in some hope. I could almost pretend this is a normal day, part of a test for our Learning.

It's nearly dark. The slope down the other side of Crocus Mountain is gentle but the path is muddy;

Tiny is carrying my basket, but Nunu is still carrying hers and leaning on me so heavily that I might as well be carrying her. Pellie's family stopped to camp when the sun set. Our family is alone.

Suddenly there are lights moving through the darkness: torches coming toward us. Dada shouts, and now the men beneath the torches are close enough to see. They stop before us, saluting with their free hands and panting.

"Captain!" says the first. "The chief sent us back for you."

There are four of them. They take the legs of my mother's bed, as gently and reverently as if she were the Lady herself, and Dada's sailors take the baskets from Nunu and me. Nunu links her arms through Ibi's and mine, and we drag her the rest of the way. Only Dada walks free, yet he moves as if his burden is heavier than anyone's.

Not far ahead, firelight glows softly through windows—though the closer we get the more tired I am, the more I'm sure I can never walk that far, and the more I long for that warmth. I didn't know it was possible to be this tired.

Dada, who's been walking beside the stretcher bed, turns back as if he hears my thoughts. He takes Nunu's arm from me, and puts his other around my shoulders. For a few moments, as we reach the farmhouse and the door swinging open to welcome us, I'm very glad to be a cared-for child again.

The chief, the Lady and their family are already

there, with another uncle of our clan, a wise-woman and her tall young apprentice, and four children sleeping on fleeces like puppies in front of the fire. It's not a small house, but already crowded.

However, the farmers welcome us, shy and proud to have so many great visitors in their home. They felt the earthmother's shaking, the husband says, but the greatest damage was an urn of goat's milk that rolled off the table and shattered. "But there'll be milk again tomorrow," he says, as if that's what matters.

The wife approaches Mama on her stretcher, starting to welcome her, as if my mother is lying down for no reason other than weariness. At the sight of her face the woman gasps and makes the sign against evil.

Nunu looks as if she's going to slap her—it's probably lucky that her old legs give way at that moment and she slides down against the wall.

"Leave the lady to us!" the wise-woman says sharply, instructing the men to carry Mama nearer the fire. "We need dry coverings—for the others too, they're all soaked to the bone."

The farmer woman scurries upstairs and returns laden with fleeces and skins clutched against the baby swell of her tunic. The wise-woman rolls the sleeping children out of the way. Together with her apprentice, me and Nunu—because Nunu struggles to her feet when she sees someone else preparing to care for Mama—the wise-woman slides my mother off the bed onto dry fleeces. The bed is flipped right way up, another soft fleece laid on the hide, and we lift Mama back onto it. The wise-woman sits by her, crooning softly as she moves her hands gently over Mama's face, head and body, never quite touching, pausing at times and frowning as if she is feeling an invisible barrier.

"Come," the apprentice tells me, untying the shoulder tie on my tunic. "We need to get you dry. You too, Old One."

"Turn around!" Nunu snaps at the men, and I realize we're going to change here, in this open room, without screens or walls; secreted by nothing but trust.

"You heard her," says Dada in his captain's voice.

Trust might be enough.

But the farmer woman stares in shock as I step out of my tunic, and then my shift, to stand naked in front of the fire.

"Did you think that the Swallow Clan grow differently from you under their skirts?" Nunu hisses at her, as the tall girl rubs me dry, clucking at cuts and bruises I haven't noticed till now.

The woman flushes, and hands me a rough woollen tunic to pull on. It's warm and heavy, falling nearly to my ankles, but I am still shivering. The apprentice drapes another fleece around me like a cloak, and turns to Nunu.

"You're injured," she says gently, because my old nurse, now that someone else is caring for Mama and me, has collapsed to the floor again. Her ankle is streaked with dried blood and swollen as fat as her thigh.

"It's nothing!" Nunu snaps.

The older wise-woman, without even turning from her work of gently oiling Mama's wounds, says, "You're no good to your lady dead. Warm yourself and heal so you can help her."

Meekly and shakily, Nunu strips. Her thigh is gashed from hip to knee, still oozing blood. *People say servants don't feel pain the same way we do—but how did she walk so far like that?*

The farmer woman, however, rallies at the sight of the wound: Nunu's tongue is sharp, but the rest of her is weak. And she looks so old, so wizened: her skinny legs with the sparse gray triangle of hair between them, the empty pockets of her breasts, and most of all, the way her face has turned the color of cold ash—this is not a woman to fear. This is another wounded creature.

She brings the wise-woman honey to seal the wound, a strip torn from an old skirt for a bandage, and a cloak to cover Nunu until her own clothes dry.

There are no more dry clothes left in this house! And the woman has spread ours to dry when any fool can see they need washing, stiff as they are with dirt and blood. And all our fine things—my father's dress cloak and tunic, my fine woven bed linens, my mother's ceremonial flounced skirt—are buried under what's left of our home. Praise the goddess I found my skirt—and now I'm glad our host set it to dry by the fire, because I'd wash it myself before I let it to go out of my sight with an unknown washing girl.

The men come in to the fire now, to strip, dry, and wrap themselves in the farmer husband's clean loincloths. My father, staring down at my mother, is suddenly the same ashen color as Nunu.

"She needs rest," says the wise-woman.

"Will she wake?"

The wise-woman makes the sign of prayer. "If the gods wish it."

The room is crowded. The Lady is in the bedchamber upstairs; Kora is with her, her children, and her maid; her husband the chief will perhaps sleep in the chamber too, but I suddenly realize that the rest of us will have to stay down here, in this one hall. All together.

The goddess quivers again, rattling pots, rolling the floor under our feet.

My heart pounds; I sway and nearly fall—*the ceiling is falling on me!*

It's as real as if it's happening; I can hear it, see it, feel it in my bones . . . but the tremor stops, and the house is unharmed.

Keep Mama safe, Great Mother, and I won't complain about sleeping like a servant!

5

The earthmother has stopped shaking, though she still belches from time to time. There's not a house in the town that hasn't been damaged. My father and the chief have been organizing all uninjured men into clean-up crews. Ibi says some of the other Swallow Clan grumble, but when even the old uncle and the chief's young son are helping stack broken walls into piles and carry bodies away for burial, there's not much they can say.

Ibi's family is safe. They are with all his wife's family in a farmhouse owned by an aunt, not such a far walk from here, though we haven't seen them. There is no time for visiting and gossip.

Dada and Ibi camp in the wreckage of our home; Dada comes back here every four nights—sleeps, eats cooked meat, brings back our gold and jewelry as they find it. Ibi goes back to his wife and baby son on a different night, but he stops here on his way, to check on Mama.

Mama slept for three days before she opened her eyes and said "fish" again. The farmer woman brought her a strip of dried tunny but Mama didn't know how to chew it, so Nunu chewed it for her and spat it gently into her mouth.

I'd barely cried till then. Awake and asleep, the demon-dreams have continued: of the floor moving beneath me, of Mama bouncing down the stairs, of the terrible crash of the house falling around me and thinking I would die like a rabbit in a forgotten trap. I'd jumped and squeaked, heart pounding, at the sound of a clattering pot or a crying child, held my breath in fear when I returned from the privy, wondering if Mama had died while I was out. My whole body felt as taut as the gut-string of a lyre—but it was the spitting food that made me cry.

My beautiful mother—
    my strong and powerful mother,
    who always knows,
    is always sure—
    now helpless as a newborn babe
    soiling her fleeces,
    being rolled, unknowing,
    for her private skin to be cleansed.
And Nunu,
    who'd nursed that long ago baby
    with her own little boy—
    dead in summer heat before he could walk—
    giving the milk from her breasts—

I know that if she could make it
she would give Mama that milk again.
Instead she chews and spits
for Mama to tongue and swallow—
and I cry and cannot stop,
not because the slimy mess
turns my stomach—
though it does—
but because the world is wrong
and I don't know how
it can ever be right again.

All our surviving valuables—my new jewelry and Mama's, most of our clothes, the golden ibex and the two bronze goats, Dada's bronze dagger and the best of our bronze cooking pans—are under Mama's bed. It doesn't seem much, especially now we've given the farmers one of the pans in thanks for the use of their home.

Although most of our own pottery vessels have been smashed, the start of next year's trading collection is still safe in its store behind the kitchen. Even more importantly, Dada says that his ship, which was damaged when the shipshed collapsed, will be ready for the start of the sailing season.

Dada doesn't talk about what they find in the ruins, but Ibi does. The first time he came back he said that the worst was bringing out the bodies of people he'd known. The next time he said the worst was finding people who were still clinging to life when the searchers found them, and died when they were moved. There were dogs that spent days barking from the top of a pile of rubble, scrabbling desperately for their buried owners; sometimes the rescuers found the people alive where the dogs were barking. Sometimes they didn't.

There's no time to build proper tombs. People are buried with grief but few grave goods and little ceremony. From the other side of the mountain, absorbed in my own misery, I can barely comprehend it. Ibi tells us of a buried family in a farmhouse: grandmother, mother, husband and baby, and I can tell he's imagining how he'd feel if it had been his own wife and son.

But the people he tells me about aren't real to me. All I can think is, *They weren't Mama*.

Though the truth is, my mother isn't Mama anymore either. She is the body that lies on the bed and sometimes says "fish", and sometimes "Nunu", though she doesn't seem to recognize the old woman looking after her as her own nurse. One day she opened her eyes and looked right at me as if she knew me, but when I touched her hand she said, "Fish!" and went back to sleep. The wise-woman says an evil ghost has taken her spirit, so we must sing it back to her body, surrounding her with words that remind her spirit of its proper home. The prayers that the wise-women chant are strong magic, the songs that have been chanted for lost spirits since time began, but the old one says that Nunu's and mine are stronger still.

"Sing her life," she says. "Sing of the life and love that only you know, the secrets that tell her spirit that she is its true home."

Nunu sings her the lullabies she sang her so many years ago.

"Lullabies!" snaps Ibi, when he hears. "She's not a baby."

"Her spirit has no age," the wise-woman says mildly. "It remembers the songs of her infancy, of being a maiden and then a mother of infants. That is a powerful time for a woman's spirit. Your mother sang these to Glaucus, and to you and Leira, and heard Nunu singing for you when she rested—they are part of her home, deep in her bones and soul."

A moment's panic: *I don't know what lullabies she sang to me!*

But that's not what the wise-woman wants of me. "Sing her your own story," she commands, as if I know exactly what that is. "Sing of your memories and the stories she's told you, and anything of your Learning that you can share here, knowing that others can hear."

She looks at Ibi. "You too."

Dada knows without being told. When he returns from the city he sits by Mama, crooning love songs that I've never heard before—their own love songs. It makes me blush, because he sings of things I'm not supposed to know yet, and that I didn't think they'd still know.

I want to sing, to help,
    but my thoughts whirl—

too many, too fast—
to find the one that will call
my mother's spirit home.
There is her anger, her sternness—
and they are part of her
but not the part I want to call.
Till I remember a song
that comes with an image of Mama
singing to the toddling girl that was me,
and even though I'm not sure
the image is true,
truth swells in it as I sing:
a song of joy, of love
from mother to daughter.
A girl-child
with first hair grown long enough
to cut this day
and offered to the goddess
in the smoke of the temple fire
as promise and plea
that the goddess,
receiving this mother's heart-gift,
will keep the girl safe
to grow to maiden and mother,
raising a line of daughters—
women to praise the goddess forever—
because without her women,
the goddess will be gone.
A song I didn't know I knew
and I don't know if
I'm remembering or creating

but maybe it doesn't matter,
because at the end
Mama stirs and smiles.
"Lei," she says,
    and that is all
    but for the moment it's a lot—
    though I want more and Mama needs it,
    so I sing again,
    words straight from my soul to my lips.
I sing of the memory
    of riding her hip—
    I know it's hers, not Nunu
    because I can see the golden necklace,
    feel the longing to touch
    the silver dragonfly hanging there,
    and the knowing that Nunu
    will slap my fingers if I do,
    or if I pat
    Mama's perfectly painted face and breasts.
With small Ibi at our side,
    we stand on the hill above the town
    amongst other women dressed in glory:
    bright flounced skirts,
    and gossamer shifts laced tight
    below proud, bare breasts.
But Mama is proudest of all—
    finer, I think, even than the Lady—
    because we are watching the fleet
    process into the harbor,
    every ship safe and present
    at the end of the season—

with my Dada the admiral leading
on the biggest, fastest ship,
and my biggest brother Glaucus
with him for the first time.
I sing of our sailing
in his garlanded ship—
papyrus flowers in elegant splendor—
with the chief and the Lady,
all of the Swallow Clan—
around the bay—
our island's great lake
where the goddess of fire
breathes and belches.
I sing of women at the well,
herdsmen with goats and oxen
from foreign lands
and the many strange things
that Dada has seen;
because Mama hasn't seen them
any more than me,
but watched their creation on our wall—
images from Dada's stories.
I sing of how I loved
to press my fingers into paints and wet plaster
but not of how Mama said no—
or of how the frescoes lie shattered
in our ruined house—
but sing of the glory
of how they used to be.
And Mama smiles again, as if she can hear.

*

On Dada's fourth visit, when the full moon of the winter solstice has shrunk to nothing then grown to a quarter again, and I've just finished my bleeding in a house with no running water or privacy, he is so weary he can hardly sit up to drink his soup. He slumps by the fire, holding Mama's hand as he tells his story. "We heard rustling in the ruins of a house in the craft quarter. No one answered when we called, which wasn't surprising after all this time, but there was more rustling and a whimper, so we started to dig."

I look at his hands, with their layers of new scabs and grazes on top of old scars. He may be admiral of our trading fleet, but he works harder than any slave. Ibi says that's why the men go on digging when hope is nearly gone. And this time they had hope. No one knew who might be in the ruin, but they were determined to get them out.

"We threw out enough rubble to fill the street again," he continues, "and the more we dug, the more whimpering we heard. Until finally," he smiles at Mama, who doesn't notice, and then at me, and I'm nearly holding my breath because I'm so desperate to hear a story with a happy ending, "we pushed away a table, and found a mother dog and her pup. We pulled them out—the mother was near death, but we gave her water—and the pup was round and healthy. A good story?" he asks, as if he were a minstrel.

"A good story," I agree, and it is. The mother saved her pup. I saved my mother. The goddess spares some and takes others, and even the Lady doesn't always know why.

The quiet moment is broken by the farmer woman shooing someone from the door. The Lady has ordered that no one asking for help should be turned away, but when my father calls out, a bone-thin, shivering black dog, with a puppy at her heels, slips through the door and collapses on Dada's feet.

I scoop up the pup, who nuzzles and licks my palm.

"Poor girl, brave girl," Dada croons, rubbing behind her ears. "She must have carried that pup in her mouth the whole way, following me."

He shouts in his captain's voice for bread and milk. "She kept her pup and herself alive all this time—we can't let her die now."

I wonder if he's thinking what I am: *If this dog can live, so can Mama.*

The mother dog attaches herself to Dada; when he heads back to town after his day of rest she follows. She leaves the puppy behind—with me.

Dada's always had dogs guarding the shipsheds and sometimes on his ships, but smelly-breathed, quarrelsome animals don't belong in a home like ours, filled with beautiful things. But now this tiny creature is whining and twining around my legs as if I'm all he has left in the world. I have to pick him up or the noise will make Mama cry too. He tucks his head under my arm and snuggles against me—he is warm and helpless, and his breath when I kiss his nose smells like his last drink of milk from his mama.

He is black as the night sky, but that's not what I name him. And I don't want to call the gods' attention to him by calling him Lucky, though he'd have to be the luckiest pup in the world. But even the most jealous gods allow hope—Nunu says it amuses them to see us hoping when there is nothing we can do against the fate they've chosen.

"Hello, Chance," I say.

The puppy squirms and licks my face with his rough pink tongue—and unlocks something deep inside me. Tears stream down my face; I'm crying harder than I've ever cried before. Nunu tells me to hush and the wise-woman tells me I'm upsetting my mother, but Chance just goes on licking the tears off my face as fast as he can until I can't help laughing. Laughing and crying together, I don't know which one it is, but I can't stop until I'm dry and empty as a seed husk, and Nunu makes me drink a cup of ale.

For the first time since the house fell down, I feel alive.

The Lady and Kora devote themselves to appeasing the great mother, filling the house with chanting and song to make up for missing the winter rites on the proper day.

Because the mother tore the town and temple apart in the hours before we could perform them!

I don't say that out loud.

The Lady sings the sun to rise each morning from the shelter of the front portico, so that the farm folk can attend as well as the household; often fishers or folk from other farms come as well, their faces lighting with joy at seeing her for themselves. After the dawn ceremony they sing over my mother and the Lady talks to her of their childhood. "You did well to save her," she tells me, kissing my forehead. Kora smiles but rarely speaks except in prayer. She doesn't seem to remember that we once played.

Every few days they command a goat to be brought for sacrifice, offering the goddess the smoke of burning bones and fat, and feeding the household with the meat. But with the farmhouse full of their household and ours, there's not much left for the folk in the animal sheds.

I've been praying too, singing Mama's spirit and beseeching the goddess to let it return—but Chance seems to have licked away a veil from my eyes. The Lady and Kora are doing the great mother's work, but the farm men have followed Dada and the chief to help dig out the town, and there aren't enough servants left to run the household. The farmer woman, whose belly is growing bigger every day, is so tired she can barely speak by sundown. Nunu is still weak and the wise-women are exhausted, yet they've all been caring for me as well as Mama.

A sudden fire burns through me. I think of Dada and Ibi, working like slaves in the ruined town, and wish I could join them. I want to rescue someone the way they rescued Chance; to pick up the shattered beams in our home and rebuild it.

That dream only lasts a moment. I'm not as strong as Ibi; I'm not even as strong as the farm girls, younger than me, who haul in buckets of water for us every day.

But I've got to do something—and now the wisewoman's apprentice is rolling Mama to her side, for Nunu to wash her.

"Let me," I say.

"Don't be ridiculous," snaps Nunu. "It wouldn't be right."

"Nothing's right anymore, Nunu!"

The young woman straightens, motioning for me to put my hand on Mama's shoulder where hers is.

It feels right to be doing this. Nunu insists on taking the soilings away herself, but I go out to the spring, Chance at my heels, and refill our pitchers with water.

As the days roll on, I take over more of the water carrying. The Lady always thanks me for carrying it up to her rooms, but she doesn't know I fetch it from the spring myself—not just for my little family and hers, but even for the farmers. I'm ashamed to tell her, and afraid she'll stop me. I'll be very glad when life goes back to how it should be and I never have to lift another bucket, but for now, despite the stench from the privies and the animal sheds, it's a relief to be out of the house for those moments. I almost envy the two farm girls who are sent out to search the fields for greens. They go even when it's raining; they're often wet and muddy—but they're together; friends. I know that Pellie and her family are safe, in a farmhouse not far from town, but I haven't seen her since the day we fled here.

A terrible groan wakes us before dawn. *The earth-mother is trembling again!* But the house is still; the scream that follows comes from the kitchen where the farmers sleep.

"The baby is coming!" the farmer husband shouts. The wise-women roll off their fleeces and are in the kitchen before I even understand what's happening.

I've never seen a birth before. I don't know if this is harder than usual, but it's long and frightening; the wise-woman's voice is calm as always but her apprentice can't keep the anxiety from hers. I realize the farmer woman, and the baby trying to be born, could die.

A birthing room is no place for a man; her husband leaves as soon he's woken the wise-women, taking the three small children with him. The youngest is still asleep but the two older ones are crying; I can still hear the wails of "Mama!" when they disappear out the door.

My own mama stirs restlessly, as if she thinks that it's her children crying.

"I'm here," I tell her, smoothing her forehead, but she keeps on struggling to get out bed, muttering, "Lei, Lei!"

"Leira's here," Nunu tells her sharply. "Nunu's here. Be a good girl and go back to sleep."

She settles better for Nunu than me.

The laboring woman moans again; the wise-woman says something to her apprentice I can't hear, then, louder, in the same tone she uses for Mama, "Rika, I want you to take a deep breath. The baby will be here soon."

Rika! I've never known her name.

Rika, who's taken in and cared for us. Rika, who loves her children as Mama loves hers, and whose children love her as I love Mama.

She mustn't die!

I pull my winter tunic on over my nightshift and go out to the kitchen. Rika is squatting, panting, with the apprentice supporting her shoulders.

"How can I help?"

"Build up the fire," says the wise-woman. "The baby will need warmth when it comes."

The fire is banked for the night, though a small log is glowing where the husband had poked it to light the torch. I'm not sure how to tend a fire, but it can't be hard. I find the smaller wood stored by the door, pile it on and poke it all with a stick till it flames. There's a lot of smoke.

When the black sky outside turns gray, then pink, and Rika is still laboring, I take our pitchers and head to the stream for water. It takes me six trips to fill the ewers for everyone, and then another two because the wise-women use theirs so quickly. The sun is up by the time I finish; I'm very hungry and don't know what there will be for breakfast, because with Rika and the wise-women filling the kitchen, no one has prepared the usual barley porridge. But there must be barley cakes stored, and the daily cheeses and yoghurt from the goats—though even that is becoming less, as it won't be long now till the goats have their own kids, and they are not making as much milk for the farmers.

A man is coming toward the house, wearing the rough kilt and cape of the fishers in winter, with octopuses dangling on a pole slung over his shoulder. He's nearly at the kitchen door when I shout.

"You can't go in there!"

He stops, but I can see that he's confused about who I am. He'd know there are Swallow Clan staying here, but he wouldn't expect them to be carrying water.

"Rika wants these octopuses," he says.

"I'll take them to her."

"She promised me four cheeses and two baskets of lentils."

Something in his face tells me he's lying. I think quickly, trying to compare the meals from the octopuses with those big cheeses that take a day's worth of milk from the flock—and I know there aren't many baskets of lentils left.

"Two cheeses," I say.

He throws his hands to his face in horror.

Maybe he was telling the truth.

But I've seen the kitchen; I've seen how much food there is, and how many people.

"You know that this house shelters the Lady and Kora, and the chief? If you cheat Rika, you cheat them."

He nods, his eyes wary.

"I will give you a bronze pot. And you will bring us octopus or other fish every day till the spring festival."

His face lights up, though he guards it quickly as he bargains. "Till the moon turns."

"Till the spring festival," I insist.

He nods again, slowly. "Goddess watch me—you will have your fish."

I carry my water pitchers inside, search under Mama's bed, pull out one of our good bronze cooking pots, and take it out to the fisher. He receives it reverently and quickly disappears down the road.

I'm trembling. Dada has traded around the world for those pots, and if the fisher doesn't keep his promise, I've given one away for six small octopuses.

But when I carry them into the kitchen, the wise-women are smiling and Rika is sitting up with a tiny, red baby at her breast. My worry turns to pride. Rika and her baby will live—and I've helped feed them.

6

Rika's baby and my puppy both grow. The baby can suckle, cry and almost lift his head. Rika carries him in a sling against her chest; he is always with her, and exhausted as she is, when she sits to feed him, her gaze is pure love.

That's the same love that kept Chance alive in the ruins, I think—but unlike Rika, who loves her older children too, Chance's mother ignores him when she returns with Dada.

"But you have me now," I whisper into his floppy ear, and he licks my face as if he understands. Chance understands a lot. Rika's husband has given me a leather collar and cord so that I can hold him back when the farm dogs are moving the sheep, but he already knows his name, and usually comes when I call him. He jumps to my shoulders with his front legs around my neck—a bad trick, says Dada, because he'll be a big dog one day. I know that's true, so I teach him the game of sitting still at my feet or waiting by Nunu. Nunu says he's a dirty ridiculous creature, but strokes his head. His head is smooth, and soothing to stroke.

"He's not much use yet," she says, "but you might as well take him when you go out for the water or washing."

I don't need to be reminded. I don't think anyone's going to attack me, but with my dog by my side I don't feel quite so alone when I see the farm girls walking in pairs.

He's not big yet: I still let him jump to my shoulders. For a few minutes at a time, holding this squirming wriggle of joy makes me forget that everything else is wrong with the world. And on these cold winter nights, a warm puppy snuggled on my feet is better than a brazier or another fleece.

Not everyone is so lucky. The rainy season goes on, wetter, colder, and longer than it has ever been. There's no indoor toilet, and the little privy house behind the kitchen garden, which is really nothing but a shelter over a wooden bench with a hole dropping to a deep pit, is filling and stinking. The folk sheltering in the animal sheds are not allowed to use it, and have dug new pits for themselves, with no seats and not much shelter.

The fisher brings us octopus, shellfish, or fish every day. If he misses one we know it's because he had nothing to bring; Dada says that I made a good trade. But the goats' milk has dried up and there are no new kids yet; the dried peas and lentils are nearly gone and the barley is getting low. Sometimes a rabbit or bird is caught in a trap; once a hunter brought the meat of a wild boar to trade, and the chief has twice shot a wild goat—but even a goat doesn't go far for so many people.

And now there is sickness. It begins with shivering and a streaming nose, then a sore throat and a cough that doesn't stop till the breath is gone and the person faints. That's when the fever comes in: the sweats and shaking and delirium. And then death.

The first dawn that we were woken by unearthly wails, Rika herself raced to the shed to investigate, returning grave but not shaken.

"It was our oldest woman servant," she said, pointing her fingers against evil. "She'd already lived past her time."

There'd been so much death already, even a young mother of our clan, and two potters at the height of their powers from Nunu's sister-in-law's workshop. The Lady and Kora went to the animal shed with a prayer to cleanse the death spirit, but we weren't disturbed by the keening when the old woman was buried that afternoon. Only Nunu, sweeping out the central room where we are still living, stopped to stand with her hand on her heart, her lips moving in a chant to the dead as the burial procession passed.

Farewell to life,
the sun and sky,

now you depart
for our mother's heart.
Farewell to toil,
to sea and soil,
for you will rest,
in our mother's breast.
Your days are done
your life here gone
the mother has chosen
you for her own.
Stay with her there
and leave us here.

Nunu sang those last lines a few times, hoping that the goddess wouldn't need another old woman for a while, but it hasn't worked. The goddess keeps wanting more, and she doesn't just want old ones. Before the moon is full again, she takes nearly everyone in the shed, and then she starts on the house.

She takes Kora late one morning, and before that same day's sunset she takes the Lady.

The wise-woman beckons me. "It's time to prepare them for the goddess."

"I haven't finished my Learning!" I protest.

"You're an almost-woman and the closest relative," she replies shortly. "The Lady's only living daughter is still a child; she has no sister, and her other two cousins cannot get here in time."

She doesn't mention Mama, except to add more gently, "I'll show you what to do, and her maidservant will help. This is part of life—and it won't be as hard as looking after your mother alone in the dark, when your house fell on you."

She is right. We do Kora first, before she stiffens, because they'd been afraid to let the Lady know that her daughter had died—though she knew, of course she knew, says the wise-woman, any mother would have known. We wash and oil her body, and I arrange her in ceremonial dress, with all her jewelry, and bind her arms and legs so that she cannot fight her fate, or flop loose on the burying board on the way to her grave. As I do it she becomes less Kora and more Gellia, the cousin I played with as a child; tears blind me as I thread her round gold hoops through the holes in her ears.

"Sorry," I say, because I've missed and stabbed her right ear. "Sorry."

But for the Lady, the fact of who she is—who she was—weighs heavier and heavier on me as we go on. Our goddess has no servant; we have no Lady and guide to our goddess.

We sit with them all the next day, keening and chanting. The room becomes crowded with women as the Swallow Clan arrive: three girls of my Learning come with their mothers, but not Pellie, whose little sister is sick, or Alia or her grandmother. Alia's leg was broken when a wall fell on it; Rastia tells me she died three days ago, and her grandmother the next day. Alia and I were not close like Pellie and me, but she was my kin, part of my life and a Learning sister; it's hard to believe she is gone, and that I hadn't even known. Rastia and I weep together, and Tullie and Chella join us.

When the men arrive, I hold my breath until I see my father and Ibi, afraid that they've died too without my knowing. I cling to Dada the way I used to when I was a child and he was about to disappear on his ship for the long sailing season.

The burial procession starts with the dawn the following morning. The chief has said they must be buried in the proper place, no matter how difficult, and the wise-woman agrees. We must pick up the pieces of our world and show the gods that we're worthy of life; that we treat her servants with respect.

As we start out, I can't help thinking of the old servant woman's death, with Nunu's brief chant the only notice from the house. Now Nunu is the only one to stay behind, to care for Mama.

When did I stop thinking of Mama as one of us? Mama and Nunu are *both* staying behind. It's just that Nunu is the only one who knows it.

The chief leads the procession, with his young daughter and his son Lius. I've never noticed before what a good-looking boy Lius is. Grief makes him seem older; he's nearly as tall as his father as he takes his little sister's hand, pulling her gently along with him. It's too bad he's younger than me . . . *How can I think that now, at the funeral of his mother and sister, my aunt and cousin, the Lady and Kora?*

It's a relief when the wise-women start keening. The high ululation unlocks the horror inside me, pulsating in my ears and throat, driving out thought, driving out everything except its own pure grief: for the Lady and Kora, for all the dead, for our beautiful city and my beautiful home in it, for my Mama, who sleeps on like a grub in a cocoon while the living die around her.

My own keening mingles with the others' till I can't hear it alone, because we are one, from Swallow Clan to slaves—all one and all emptied, hollowed out by grief and sound. The little girl stumbles back to me, trying to wail through her tears, and I take her hand while Lius joins his father, taking his turn at banging the bronze shield gong all along the way.

The sun rises behind us as we reach the top of Crocus Mountain. The slopes brighten to green grass, white rock and red clay; the sea shimmers from dawn gray to early morning blue. Even the town, when it first comes into view, looks normal and right, as if we're on our way home.

But it's not normal or right, and we're not going home. We keep on the path past the stink of the purple works, on to the bend where Triangle Plaza and the roof of our home should be clear to see.

Dada, Ibi, and the chief have talked of all the work that's been done. I've seen from their gray faces and sweat-stained, filthy tunics that they've worked as long and hard as anyone could, for the cycle of two full moons. I thought the town would be starting to look whole again—not quite perfect, but like a room that needs sweeping.

It's still a pile of stones and brokenness. It's worse than I remembered, much worse than I've imagined. I can't pick out the Plaza, the temple, the Lady's House or ours. It's not home at all, and if I wasn't already keening I'd be screaming now. It's a relief to veer east to the cemetery before we reach the outer houses, because I don't want to see any more of what used to be my home. The voices crescendo behind me as the other women reach the bend and see the ruins, and I'm fiercely glad to hear it. It would be beyond bearing to see and feel this misery alone.

It's true, the wailing says, *it's true*, the gong beats, *this pain is true, this terror is true, we all feel it, we all see it: the gods have betrayed us and everything terrible is true.*

Even the little lamb, carried over the farmer's shoulder, starts to bleat as if it knows its fate.

But when the ritual is done, when the Lady and Kora have been laid in their graves—two more graves in the midst of so many, but a more terrible loss than a thousand of those common mounds—when their gifts of gold and bronze, honey and oil have been placed with them before the earth covers them forever, when the chief slits the lamb's throat and the blood spurts onto the fresh dirt, feeding the great mother, the goddess of earth and death, in the hope that she will care for them and for us—I wonder how this one little lamb will be enough, when she has already taken more people than we can count.

7

"The ship is ready," Dada is saying.

It's the news I've been dreading. This long winter is ending, and the coming full moon will be the spring festival and the start of the sailing season.

Pellie's mother will celebrate it as the new Lady; Pellie's older sister is the new Kora. The chief announced them after the burials, when our faces were still streaked with the mud of mourning and the blood of the lamb, but the Swallow Clan had decided it together. Pellie and I held hands as we listened with our sister Learners.

There wasn't much discussion. As the wise-woman told Nunu when we returned, "By the lines of birth and breeding it would be your mistress, but . . ." She gestures at my mother, sleeping curled like a baby on her bed, and is kind enough not to go on.

I've never wanted to be Kora—I've never thought about it—why would I? But now rage bubbles, sick as the stench of a goddess burp, because if Mama were well and could have taken her proper role, I'd have become Kora—and one day, the Lady.

Instead, it's another thing that's gone with Mama's accident.

The chief will stay the chief, but Pellie's mother won't put her husband aside to marry him. They are still in a farmhouse on the town side of Crocus Mountain. It's even more crowded than here—and although Pellie's little sister has recovered, they've had deaths from the sickness there too. The chief says he will move his household when the sickness ends, but for now, the chief and the Lady are not in the same home, and the world seems as crooked as a broken pot stuck together with reeds and fresh clay. The two sides meet, but the mend shows, and the pot always leaks.

Now Dada and Ibi will be leaving. My world will break a little bit more.

And the goddess is belching every few days, reminding us that more change is coming.

"Leaving," says Dada, and I can't hear more,
    as if the sea that will take him
    is already roaring between us.
To be alone with Nunu and Mama
    in this house of strangers—
    because though Rika is kind,
    grateful for my help
    and lets me hold her baby,
    she's too conscious of my status

to remember I'm a girl,
and the wise-women,
only one rung down
and known in my life before,
have time for nothing but illness
and exhausted sleep.
"Do you hear me?" asks Dada.
    "We will take your mother
    from this place of illness and death
    to the palace of Tarmara
    in the Great Island where Glaucus stays.
    The wise-women there will heal her
    if the goddess wills it."
"What about me?" I wail,
    like a child afraid to be alone.
    "Will I go to Pellie and the Lady?"
    Because the coming of spring
    will be the next season of Learning
    and I still haven't learned
    the rites of midwinter.
A sudden comfort—
    no matter how crowded the house,
    how ill the servants
    or how strange it will be
    to call her sister Kora,
    being with my friend
    is like a wish from another life
    that will make this one
    easier to bear.
"Stay with Pellie?" my father roars,
    with his voice from the sea,

"Desert your mama?
       You'll come with us,
       and watching over her,
       you'll grow strong
       and beautiful again—
       better to wait for womanhood
       than to die learning."
This house has no mirrors
       but in my father's voice I see
       how thin I've grown,
       broken-nailed and grimed,
       smelling like a slave.
His voice changes, and as if in a song,
       he tells of the town,
       near in beauty to our own
       with wise-women as skilled as ours
       in rooms of comfort,
       food and herbs to spare,
       as we once had.
The same gods reign—
       their earthmother a sister to our own,
       the small gods of rivers and trees
       are cousin-kin;
       we speak the same tongue,
       worship the same way,
       and most of all—
       my brother will be there,
       wise in the ways of the court.
"And you," I say, but Dada smiles sadly,
       "The land needs its trade.
       We must go on around the sea,

buying what we can
with what we've sold,
to return in autumn
with wealth to rebuild."
But he has no answer
to how I will complete my Learning
or become a woman,
except to say again
that if the goddess wants me to serve
and bear children to serve in their turn
she needs me to live.
"Sometimes," says Dada,
"even the gods have to change to survive."
Part of me thinks
that it's easy for him to say
because he's already a man
and so are his sons
but another part is filled
with excitement and hope
that Mama will be well
and we will live as we ought:
safe, comfortable
and even happy.

Mama's wounds are mostly healed now; she looks like
herself. She can sit up. With someone at her side she
can stand while her bed is cleared, and with two people
she can move from her bed to a chair or squat over a
chamber pot. She says "yes-yes-yes" and "no-no-no",
and though she sometimes gets them backwards if
she grows too excited, we can always tell which she

means. For everything else she says, "Fish." We know now it doesn't mean fish—except sometimes at dinner. Sometimes she gets angry when we don't understand, and shouts, "Fish, fish, FISH!" louder and louder, as if we're just not listening properly. Other times she looks sad, as if she understands that she isn't making sense, and murmurs it over and over, "fish, fish, fish, oh fish, fish, fish." But most of the time she seems quite happy, chattering like a baby. "Fish?" she'll ask, and when I say, "Yes, Mama," she smiles and repeats it.

It's hard to say "yes" and smile when your mother is talking nonsense. I can't always do it. "No, Mama, Chance is a puppy, not a fish! You want to pee, not fish!"

Then Mama cries, and Nunu—sharp-tongued, cranky Nunu—soothes her, murmuring and stroking her back. She's very good at sounding gentle while her tongue whips this ungrateful daughter, this girl who is not yet a woman and it's just as well because she's not ready to be a mother if she can be so cruel, and would she scold her puppy if it didn't understand?

But Mama's not a puppy or a baby, and she's not an ancient woman without teeth or wits. She's a broken spirit living in my mother's body.

We've sung to that broken spirit for nearly three moon cycles, and it hasn't healed yet. Dada is right— we have to take her somewhere else.

But ships can't sail till after the full moon of the spring festival. The moon is barely at the half now, not a quarter of the way through the cycle; I'll be here for that next step of my Learning.

I wake to greet the dawn with him; we don't sing it as Mama or the Lady would, but stand together, hands on hearts to watch the sun rise from the sea, before sharing bread and a cup of wine-milk.

"I'll finish the loading of the ship," he says. "The men will stay behind to carry your mother more slowly. Pack everything except the pot I gave our hosts. We'll sleep at the shipshed and sail at dawn."

"Dawn *tomorrow*?"

He nods, trotting out his old saying, "The gods choose the weather and we must follow."

"But you've always said that's why the sailing season is when it is—the gods chose the weather between the spring festival and the autumn, and you follow within it."

"This time we follow outside it."

There's more he's not telling me, but I know Dada too well to go on asking.

Nunu will come with us, of course, but Dada gives the young maid Tiny and an older manservant the choice—the man says he'll try his luck as a sailor, but I've seen Tiny with one of the goatherds, so I'm not surprised that she decides to stay on the farm. What I am surprised about is Dada giving them a choice. I thought he might have given them to the farmers and saved the bronze pot.

"I don't want people on the ship who don't want to be there," he says.

The other surprise is that Ibi plans to bring his wife

and baby son. He's with them now, and will meet us at the shipsheds. The farmhouse they're staying in had little damage, and though it's overcrowded, I don't think they've had much sickness. I ask if they will stay in Tarmara with us, but Dada isn't sure.

"We'll worry about getting everyone there first," he says, and out of all these strange things—going outside the sailing season, giving servants a choice, taking Ibi's family as well as ours—this is the strangest of all. Dada's voyages are planned down to the last detail: not just when the gods decree the time is right, but also exactly what crew, what cargo, what provisions. "The gods will throw us plenty of surprises along the way," he always says, "but it pleases them if we start off with care."

Now he's rushing, the ship barely prepared, the season not started, unknown passengers taking up good cargo room . . .

It takes longer to pack and ready ourselves than I expected. We've lived on the farm for nearly a season, and the valuables and possessions Dada's unearthed from the house fill many baskets. Tiny and I have shaken the dust from the clothes—the fine embroidered shifts and the swallow dance fishnet shawl—that are too fine to wear here. She cries as she helps me pack; she's been in our household since she was old enough to work, four or five years—she's about the same age as me, though she's still so little. But now she's free, ready to start her new life with the goatherd, becoming a woman while I am still a maiden.

I give her one of my old tunics; she cries more, and so do I, just a little.

I'll wear a tunic on the ship, but once we get to the town—*Tarmara*, I practice saying—I will need only my finery. For today I'm dressed as I was for the saffron gathering, half a year ago, with every piece of jewelry that I own and some of Mama's bracelets—she likes the feeling of them on her left arm, but plucks restlessly at the one on her right, till I'm afraid she'll throw it off along the way. I'm wearing my cloak and new sandals, though. The cobbler lost his workshop in the shaking, but has been busier than he's ever been, making new sandals for everyone who lost theirs under the rubble. They are stiffer than my old ones; the toe thong rubs on my left foot.

Mama will be travelling the same way she did the terrible day that we fled here, carried on her upside-down bed, but Nunu has painted her face as well as mine: eyes, lips and rouged cheeks. Dada brought the make-up back on this last visit: "Use it," he'd ordered. "The priest-folk are travelling, the sailing season opening early, bringing trade and prosperity back to the island—the people need to see the procession."

And a procession it is. There's barely an able-bodied person left on the farm for the day. I lead, Chance trotting beside me, followed by Dada's four men carrying Mama's stretcher, Nunu and the wise-women by her side. Rika has a lamb over her shoulders and her man a goat, sacrifices for our safe journey; behind them servants carry our baskets and provisions. I carry nothing but a bag with the extra earrings—the only jewelry I couldn't wear—and our small gold ibex, our most precious possession.

We follow the meandering godpath over the mountain. The first wildflowers splash reds and purples in the green; springs bubble clear and fresh after the winter rains, and the grass is lush. There's no hymn for a captain's wife and daughter crossing from the wrong side of the mountain to set sail with him, and it's not yet time for the spring songs, so we sing thanks to the goddess for the rain that's fallen, and more thanks that it's not falling today.

"Visit each shrine, each god on the path—a libation and a prayer for our safe return," Dada had ordered, not caring that I don't know the prayers yet.

"Speak with your heart and the goddess will hear," says the wise-woman.

> My heart sings of its love
>> for my land of steep cliffs,
>> gray, brown, and red;
>> rocky hills where wild goats leap
>> and swallows fly home to nest;
>> snug, safe harbors
>> and the small steaming islet
>> where the great mother
>> meets the god of the sea.
> How I fear to leave
>> and already long to return.

I sing
    to the rock god who stands
    overlooking the town,
    the goddess of the stream
    that never runs dry,
    the god of winds at the narrow rock path
    and the goddess of childbirth
    in the wishing tree—
    I understand much
    that I didn't before,
    and by Tiny's blushes
    know she's prayed at this tree
    and understand why she must stay.

By the time we reach town, my soul is full and peaceful.
I know that I've sung the island for Mama the best that I
can. Nunu is smiling and so are the wise-women. We
manage to keep smiling as we start through the town,
because it's not such a shock this time. *Is that how
Dada and the chief keep going? Can we can get used to
anything, no matter how terrible it is?*

    I don't start shaking till we meet Dada at the ruins
of our house. All this time, I've tried not to think of
that day; now I can't stop. I seem to be back at the
bottom of the stairs as Mama tumbles and the house
crashes. The fear presses on my chest, stops my throat,
blacks out my eyes.

    Dada steadies me with an arm. "We must farewell
the spirit of the house."

    With Chance trembling at my side, I pick my way

over the rubble to the hole at the back of the kitchen where the house snake lives.

I pour her a libation of wine and a sprinkle of grain.

"We leave you this gift," says Dada, "as a token of our hope to return."

Carefully, he places the golden ibex into a chest and slides it into a hole under the floorboards, behind the cupboards.

The men pick up Mama's stretcher, and we leave our home.

8

It's a short walk to the harbor, but folk have come back from wherever they've been staying to watch us, and it's late afternoon when we arrive.

The shipsheds have been cleared and the storage rooms are secure and full. Over the last weeks Dada has managed to find enough undamaged pottery to start his trading season, some from the stores under our house, and much from Nunu's sister-in-law's workshop. Nunu loses her look of terror and almost bristles with pride when she recognizes the men loading the precious cargo.

The ship is already at the top of the slipway. The rowers' benches and high, curving bowsprit have been repaired but there was no time to repaint the swallows on the left side, where the shipshed's roof beam landed. Dada's high steering chair is in place at the stern, and the cabin awnings are rolled up so that I can see the chairs in place, and the bed for Mama. It does not look like a very big place to spend a long time.

Sailors, porters, and workers bustle, stowing provisions and sorting cargo. It's the first thing that's been normal about this day—I could almost pretend that the sailing season has started, the fleet has been blessed, and this ship is the last to leave before the foreign ships arrive with their own wares to trade.

Nunu's sense of smell isn't as good as mine. It takes her a minute before the stench overwhelms her smile. Mama, who's slept on her stretcher since leaving town, coughs and sits up, waving the stink away with such a natural gesture that for an instant it seems a miracle.

"Fish," she says petulantly, waving her hand again. "Fish."

Which could almost be right, if the fish were long dead. It's the purple-dyers, three men and a woman, laden with heavy bundles. They stand well back from us, but closer than I've ever seen them. They are small and wiry, their backs bent under the weight of their loads, hands stained purple and feet grimed and tough as goat hoofs. It seems a kind of blasphemy that although they barely look human, the men's loincloths and the woman's skirt are splashed with the sacred color.

"The goods have been properly aired?" my father demands.

Their leader speaks, but is so nervous that I can't understand his answer. My father nods and his men take the bundles, screwing their faces in disgust.

The packs my father opens to inspect are fine linen, shaded from the soft pink of sunrise to the deepest royal purple, dark as the sea at sunset. Only the faintest sea-scent lingers. I can feel Dada's sigh of relief: this fabric is the highest quality, and will trade well. It's a good omen for a desperately needed trading season.

He nods, and the dyers disappear quickly, carrying their stink with them.

We camp in the emptied storerooms, and are ready at dawn when the Lady, the chief and all the able-bodied Swallow Clan arrive at the harbor. Many of our entourage have sheltered with us overnight; now folk flock to the quay again—it's crowded, lined with people back up the banks of the inlet almost to the town itself.

Up to our house, I think, and imagine the view in reverse, the way I've so often seen it from the windows of my father's room.

The ship on the slipway seems taller now that I'm about to board. The different layers of my ceremonial shift and skirt should let me get on decorously, without showing my secret women's parts—but I avoid looking at the boys of my clan behind their parents.

They might all have chosen, have been chosen, by the time I return and finish my Learning. All the rules have changed—so just for an instant, when Lius looks right at me, I look back.

Dada lays the lamb on the sacrificial stone at the top of the slipway. The chief cuts its throat with his sharp bronze knife, and the Lady catches the flowing blood.

She lifts the bowl with a prayer to the sea gods, and pours the blood over the bow of the ship.

She is so completely the Lady that I don't even think of her as Pellie's mother. She's wearing her own sacred skirt and shift, but the Lady's necklace hung with dragonflies and ducks: sun-gold, moon-silver, and the sky-blue of lapis lazuli. But it's more than that—the goddess has visited her, invested her with power and mystery, inhabited her. Her voice is the Lady's voice.

The goat's lifeless body joins the lamb's on the sacrificial rock; his blood splashes over the ship's bow. The crowd stands silent, hands on hearts until the Lady's prayer is finished. *Don't stop!* I will her, because as long as she's praying we don't have to leave.

Pellie is standing behind her sister, the new Kora. Our eyes meet, and when the prayer finishes we rush to each other, hugging tight. The saffron around our eyes streams down our faces like blood.

"I'll be back," I whisper. "It's just till the end of the sailing season."

"But your Learning!" Pellie sobs, as if she's the one being left out. "How can I finish mine without you here? How can I choose a boy without talking to you?"

I pull my favorite bracelet off my wrist and push it onto hers. "Let this talk to you from me."

"And this for you," she says, doing the same.

"Loading!" shouts Dada. *In his captain's voice,* I think, and shudder, because I'm about to discover what being on a ship means.

Pellie and I hug as if we'll never see each other again.

Dada straps Mama and her bedding into one of the leather slings used for hauling heavy cargo on board, and swings himself on deck to supervise. The men pull her up so gently—two guiding from the ship, leaning down till it seems only their toes are gripping the deck, two more on the ground fending off any bumps, and two hauling—that she doesn't even brush against the ship's hull before Dada is receiving her and carrying her to the cabin himself. Nunu is hauled up next—without any of the guidance or ceremony. Finally I'm lifted, with my puppy on my lap, dangling free for a moment like a happy child on a swing. It deposits me on the deck, and I scramble out as gracefully as I can without dropping Chance.

The ship takes me by surprise by shifting slightly as more cargo is slung up on the other side, and the puppy yelps. "Shush!" I order him. His mother follows Dada like a shadow, but never makes a sound—I don't want the sailors thinking Chance will be trouble.

Ibi's family should be next, I think.

Then I see them. Ibi's wife is leaning on his shoulder and sobbing; she's wearing the loose gown of pregnancy, but even from here I can see her chest heaving. Her family surrounds her and though they have offerings of flowers and wine, there are no bags or chests of belongings. Ibi is holding his son so tightly the child is screaming; his wife's mother is tugging at Ibi's arm, trying to get him to let the baby go.

They're not coming. He thought he'd talked her into it, but she's changed her mind, or her mother's changed it for her.

I don't blame her! Only a fool would take a baby and a woman about to give birth on a voyage.

Or someone desperate. Someone who believes that his family's fate will be worse if they stay.

A belch from the goddess, like a comment. We're so used to it these days that no one seems to notice, but Ibi's son coughs, a hiccupping cough that mixes with his screams, and turns him redder still. It breaks the spell on Ibi; he hands the baby back to his wife, farewells her as formally as a visiting dignitary, and strides back to the ship.

There is more going on than I've been told. Dada says that Mama and I are leaving because it's Mama's only chance to be healed, but I'm sure it's not the only reason.

I've watched this ritual
    every year of my childhood;
    sailed on the flower-decked ship
    in safe celebration around the cradled sea
    with the other ships behind us.
But today has no flowers
    or celebratory tours;
    the sacrifices are real
    but the ceremony a shadow —
    a children's game
    played in deadly earnest —
    the Lady not the Lady,
    the chief still bearing scars of mourning,
    subdued cheers of a bewildered people —

and the fleet not following,
for the other ships will wait
till repairs are finished
and the season right.
Sitting straight on my cabin chair,
serene as the Lady herself,
I sing sailors' responses to the people's farewell;
the ship glides on its rollers
down the slip to the sea,
and two by two the last sailors
swing themselves to the deck,
each to their place and paddle,
smooth as a dance—
and my light voice is lost
against their deep bass.
I seem to have shrunk
in this ship's world of men
where my father is chief
and there is no Lady.
With a lift and a roll,
the ship slides free;
my father on his throne
shoves the steering oar
and the men's paddles pull us
away from our land
till the wind god answers with his breath.
Now our square sail
pulls stronger than paddles
and the people's song fades
like a sigh in the breeze.

I swear I won't cry,
	but as I wipe the sea spray from my eyes,
	I stare at the sky—
	I don't want much,
	just one swallow,
	the first of its flock, returning for spring—
	an omen that we
	will also return.
But though gulls cry and wheel,
	hoping for fish,
	the sky is empty of what I want.

When our homeland disappears from sight, the world is empty too. The ship, which seemed so big on land, is small on this unending sea with its hidden monsters and angry gods. The fifty-two sailors, seated two by two on their benches, have lifted and stored their paddles; they sing, doze, and play knuckles as if they are relaxing in their own homes. I want them to be alert, to row and help the sail to get us to Tarmara as fast as we can. This is not like sailing around the cradled waters of home, with land in sight on every side. That was exciting; this is frightening.

Dada calls Ibi to take the steering paddle, and runs lightly down the center walk-bridge to the cabin. Mama is sleeping, Nunu dozing at her feet. Chance has finally stopped whining and fallen asleep on my lap.

"Is that dog not too big for laps?" Dada asks.

"I didn't want him to wake Mama with his crying."

"Ah," says Dada. "I was confused—I didn't realize it was the pup that needed comforting."

My face burns, but Dada pretends not to notice.

He strokes Mama's hair off her face; pulls the coverlet up over her shoulders. "Change into your travelling clothes," he says, "and come out on deck with me. Your mama will be safe here with Nunu."

Dropping the awnings for privacy and shade, he turns his back to me, and continues gently stroking Mama's forehead while I undo my wrapped skirt, exchange my embroidered red shift for a plain one, and pull a warm woollen tunic on top. The excitement of putting on my ceremonial maiden's dress yesterday wore off long before we reached town; my season on the farm has taught me how much freer a tunic can be. And warmer.

"Come," says Dada, and I follow him out of the cabin, duck under the square sail and past the rows of sailors, up the central bridge to the raised deck of the bow.

Dada's eyes sweep the horizon. I think he's going to show me something, but all he does is smile and say, "Breathe. Close your eyes, feel the wind and breathe."

So I do. My bare feet grip the wooden deck, and now that I can't see the great emptiness of sea and sky, I feel the breeze and salt spray fresh on my face like a gift. Its energy fills me and washes away the constant worries and fears. My body shifts with the rocking of the ship.

I open my eyes to see a parade of flying fish burst free from the waves, a family of dolphins close behind them. When the fish disappear, the dolphins return to the ship, leading us on our way.

9

Though the sea has lost the terrors
    of empty vastness,
    a day and a night
    seem to last a full moon.
    The rocking ship
    makes Nunu throw up
    so I have to care for my maid
    as well as my mother
    while I would rather stand on deck
    to watch for birds
    and land.
The Great Island is well named—
    we see it early, from far away.
    Too wide across, says Dada,
    to see the ends;
    not as beautiful as my home,
    but with flatlands between hills
    and white-headed mountains,

not as strange
as some of Dada's stories.
I can't yet see the harbor
but Dada calls me
to leave Mama and Nunu
and stand with him at the steering oar;
so as the sail drops
and the men pick up their oars
I see the channels,
the quays and shipsheds
of Tarmara Town.
Lightning excitement
flashes through me
because though the ships and harbor
are almost familiar
they are new and strange—
and I am standing by my father
seeing it all.
Beyond the quays
the town spreads,
smaller than ours, but with a great palace
as if, says Dada,
all the Swallow Clan houses
were joined with the temple
in one great, many-roomed building—
though they have no Swallow Clan here
so the rulers are priest-folk.
Here Sarpedon their chief
stores goods coming in for taxes,
sorts and trades them

and rules the land all around,
while their Lady
serves their goddess.
And my brother Glaucus—
so much older than me
he was almost a man before I was born—
lives with this chief and Lady
and I can't imagine
how sad he will be
about our Mama's lost spirit—
or how surprised to see me.
Even the wharf men are shocked
at a ship so early—
though they know Dada's sail,
and that we come in peace—
so they rush to the quays
to haul us in.
In ceremonial clothes and paint,
I cover restless Mama in her nightshift;
a coverlet embroidered
with the swallows of our land
and the ducks and dragonflies of our clan.
Once again, Dada straps her
securely to her bed,
guides it swinging to the wharf,
while Nunu mutters a prayer
giving thanks for dry land.
But when I alight in turn
the rock quay sways as if it were a boat
and Dada whispers,

"You'll get your landlegs soon—
    walk tall, representing our home."
He asks for a runner to send for my brother
    but there is something strange
    in the wharfman's accent—
    I can hardly understand his reply:
    "You must see Sarpedon, the chief."
Dada says they speak our language,
    but it's not quite right.
"I'm honored," says Dada,
    and to me: "Glaucus will be away,
    gathering goods for trade.
    He wouldn't expect us so soon."
    For though Dada always meets the chief,
    Glaucus usually runs
    to the quay to greet him.
There's no music or flowers
    to greet a captain from far away
    and our procession is small:
    the four sailors at the corners
    of Mama's upside-down bed,
    four more behind, each with a gift—
    an amphora of dark red wine,
    a pendant of two golden bees
    holding their precious comb,
    a tunic of the deepest purple
    and a fine, swallow-painted pot—
    but Dada marches in front
    with me by his side,
    trying to walk tall,

as if this long street from quay to palace
is as familiar as my own.

The palace goes on forever:
    columns, walkways and stairs;
    sacred horns on the wide flat roofs—
    a whole town
    joined into one.
A guard greets my father,
    sends a runner to the chief;
    calls a servant to pour water
    to wash our hands
    and dry them with linen—
    just as we'd do
    for a guest in our home.
The chief and Lady greet us in their chamber,
    and when my father salutes
    Sarpedon rises from his throne:
    "I am sorry for your troubles."
"Have you heard so much already?" asks my father.
    "The island will be well again
    and win the favor of the gods,
    but it suffers now
    and our healers are overwhelmed;
    from the bonds of our friendship
    I ask to entrust my wife
    to your wise-women
    and for my daughter to join my son."
The Lady is already bending over my mother,
    calling a servant for wise-women,

but Sarpedon's face pales to say "no"
    even as his words say, "My friend."
"You haven't heard:
    our great mother shook too,
    a column toppled in the courtyard
    where young men played a board game.
    Three were killed,
    and one was your son.
    We buried him with honor
    with our own dead."
"No, no, no!" my mother screams,
    and I wonder at the gods' cruelty
    that lets her understand her son's death
    when it seems she's heard nothing
    for this last bitter season.
The warrior in my father
    checks private grief in this hall of state
    though his face is as gray
    as our pebbled beach at dawn.
    "With your leave we will go now
    to the city of the dead
    and not speak of trade till morning."
"Leave your wife in my care," the Lady says kindly,
    but Dada says no,
    Mama has heard enough—
    she must say her own farewell.
I want to scream *No!* like Mama
    but stay still like Dada,
    tears washing away my careful paint
    as the world spins around me—

we left a place of death
to be greeted by death here.
And through the pain runs the thought,
What happens to us now?
Do I stay here, a not-yet-woman,
with my spirit-gone mother
and ancient maid?
But how could we live on Dada's ship
all this long trading season?
Dada takes ash from the hearth,
streaks his face and Mama's;
Ibi and I do the same,
and Nunu and the sailors,
then we follow a priest
to the hill of the dead
where my brother Glaucus—
dead all this time that we've thought of him,
planned for him, counted on him—
lies buried.

Sarpedon buried Glaucus with all his treasures and
weapons; there was nothing for us to do except offer
another sacrifice, letting the lamb's blood soak through
the ground to feed him, even as he drank our tears and
knew we remembered him.

Back in the palace guest rooms, our faces and chests
still streaked with the ashes of grief, Dada finally tells
me the truth of why we left home.

He had taken a lamb to the new Lady to sacrifice
and ask if Mama would live. He recites the oracle's
prophecy to me now.

In pain the goddess cries
    for the swallow who comes no more
    in this dark change
    of chaos and death.
Cry the swallows
    cry the land
    cry the changes to come.
Great mother's pain
    labor of childbirth
    labor of death;
    from her belly
    spews the dark.
Swallows flee
    swallows fly
    swallows come no more
    yet live again.

The Lady—Pellie's mother—said that it meant
Mama would die, and the goddess was grieving for
all those who had died in the shaking and the winter
illness that came after.

Dada thought she was wrong. Gods don't grieve for
humans, he says. Our years are short; we all return to
the great mother at some time—the gods don't care if
it's sooner or later. But weak as mortals are, the gods still
need us to feed them the smoke and blood of sacrifice.

"The gods will only grieve when no mortals are left,"
he says now. "That's why I believed we must flee like
the swallows in autumn—the swallows who haven't
yet returned for the spring."

"Can a man read—" I stop myself, but Dada answers anyway.

"Can a man read the goddess's prophecy? I don't know. But I prayed to the god of the sea, whose ways I understand better, and it seemed that he was calling me back to serve him."

"And?" says Ibi, almost angrily. "Tell her the rest."

My father sighs. "And I had a dream. A demon-dream, but it felt like a true one, of the great mother birthing fire and darkness to cover our land. That's why Ibi wanted his family to come. That's why we brought everyone who would; why I have told the other ships to follow as soon as they can."

"But the Lady is the Lady," Ibi growls, "and we couldn't defy her."

"And I'm a priest only in clan," says Dada. "I've been at sea all my life. What do I know of prophecies? Besides, our ships are small compared to the land—if we'd shared my dream, how would we take the people who wanted to flee?"

"But your dream didn't tell you that Glaucus was already dead," Ibi snaps. "Perhaps the Lady was right, not the sea captain."

"More than likely," says Dada. "But I couldn't stay and watch the gods take your mama, just to prove it."

After three days of mourning, Dada says we must begin to sell the trade goods, and look for more to buy for his next stop.

"But we need a trading ambassador here," he adds.

Ibi's as cantakerous as a wild boar, and rage about leaving his wife behind has only burned brighter since we learned of Glaucus's death—but I'm glad he'll be staying with us.

"Be courteous to all and trust no one," Dada continues. "Sarpedon and the Lady are courteous hosts, but their loyalty is to their own land, their own gods and the people who serve them—just as yours are to the Isle of Swallows."

I suddenly realize he's talking to me.

"*I* can't be an ambassador! Why not Ibi?"

"I can't stay on land," says Ibi. "Dada's dream haunts me every night. It's only at sea that I can sleep and forget my family for moments at a time."

"But I haven't even finished my Learning!"

"You'll learn more in one season at this palace than in three seasons of Learning."

I keep on spluttering, but my exclamations wash over my father's ears like the cooing of doves.

"Think of it this way," he says finally, "if your Mama's spirit hadn't wandered, she'd be the Lady now, and you'd become Kora at the end of your Learning. This is a time of change: in this new place, you'll become a woman and serve our gods by honoring our home. You'll have goods to trade, and to gift as seems wise; you'll speak to our sailors and wandering craft-folk with the voice of the Swallow Clan—our Kora in this land."

He holds my face in his hands, looking into my eyes so that I can't look away.

"I'll return next spring with the swallows."

*

But first, Dada says, he'll teach me all that he can. I go around the palace with him and Ibi in their trading.

"There are many times in life when you need to appear more confident than you are," says Dada. "Trading is not one of them. Let the traders see you as a child—then shock them with your sharpness."

So I stand back, Chance pressed close to my side, and watch Dada and Ibi play the bargaining game: flattering when they want to sell, walking away when they want to buy. In normal times they would simply exchange the goods that the trade ambassador has collected, with new things for him to sell. But Glaucus was the ambassador and Glaucus is dead. These are not normal times. Ibi is impatient and angry; Dada wears his grief like a cloak that he can remove briefly when he must.

The palace is so big because it's not only the home of the priest-folk and temple, but the public meeting place and craft quarter as well—and everything to do with taxation and trade.

"It's all tightly controlled by the priest-folk," says Dada. "The palace takes part of everything in taxes, whether it's goats or gold. They store farmers' produce, legislate what craft-folk produce, and control where slave labor will go."

I try to imagine Nunu's sister-in-law being told how to shape her pots. She'd be crankier than Nunu on a hot day.

The craft quarter is just across the courtyard from the guest rooms: potters, seal-stone makers, jewelers, carpenters, spinners, weavers, spear makers, bronze workers for weapons and others for art. They're all next to each other in a maze of narrow streets, with their workspaces in front of their storerooms, and their homes on top. It feels alive the way our town used to, bustling with noise and color; the heat of kilns and forges, the clanging of hammers, the singing of workers and the smell of their sweat mixed with the stink of melting copper and the scent of sea—and I hope the goddess can't hear me thinking that all of it is better than the smell of her belching.

That night Dada introduces me to Sarpedon and the Lady again, formally, as the replacement for Glaucus. Sarpedon says that our sister-countries hardly need representation from one to the other, and the Lady asks if I'm a full woman yet.

"Almost," I say, and she smiles and says she will watch over me like her own child.

"I don't trust that one," Nunu says when we're alone.

"She's the Lady!"

"Lady of this land, not ours. Did you see her eyes widen with gladness when you said you were still a maiden? You think she's happy because she needs more children to care for? She's got five of her own! She thinks that if you haven't finished Learning, she can guide you however she wants."

The problem with Nunu is that she thinks everyone's as crabby as she is.

The Lady—who truly is kind and welcoming, no matter what Nunu says—has given us Glaucus's room in the palace. Dada and Ibi are still in the guest rooms but Mama, Nunu and I have moved in to where we'll live till they return. The wise-women visit Mama every day.

And Mama is getting better. Her spirit is still wandering, but her body is stronger. For two days after we heard that Glaucus was dead, she did nothing but cry and sleep; every time she woke up she looked around as if she knew us, before remembering that her son was dead and starting to wail all over again. While she wails, she walks, round and round our room in circles—it's hard to believe that when we were at the farmhouse we could barely get her out of bed to take a few steps. Now we can hardly stop her walking and the wise-women give her poppy juice at night to make her sleep. Even better, she only cries in the morning; by the time the sun is high her tears dry and she just walks, her eyes empty as a painted picture's.

Sometimes I think that her body is getting ready to welcome her spirit home and that soon she'll be my Mama again.

Other times I think that her wandering spirit met Glaucus's when he died, and will stay with him always.

The Tarmaran trade priest says that Glaucus hadn't started collecting merchandise before he died.

"And the goods we left him with, to start his trading?" Dada asks. "He had a quantity of swallow pots and purple cloth—do you know where we could find them?"

The trade priest shakes his hand in a strange rolling movement, as if he's throwing dice. "Gone long before," he says sadly.

Ibi stiffens, but Dada salutes and glares at Ibi till he does too. "I am sorry for any care he cost you," he says, and motions us to follow him out of the courtyard and the gate.

He may have apologized, but anyone who knows my father can see the rage in his stiff-legged walk. None of us speak till we're on the path to the hill of the dead, well away from the palace and out of earshot of anyone at all.

Ibi's the first to burst. "Glaucus gambling! It's a lie!"

"Of course it's a lie," Dada snaps. "And a lie against the dead is a lie against the gods. That's why he hasn't met us sooner. But we are guests in Tarmara, and I don't know if Sarpedon and the Lady know of the lie. It's not easy for a guest to tell a chief that his trade priest is a liar and a thief—and until we can, I don't want the priest to suspect that we know. That's why I didn't ask about the gold and bronze: Glaucus had two small daggers and four sets of gold earrings."

His voice breaks, harsh as a raven, when he says his son's name. When he turns to me, his eyes are desperate. "We have no choice. Your mama cannot sail with us; you need to stay with her. But I won't be leaving you with as many goods as I'd wish, and most importantly, not with the trust I'd wish. Sarpedon and the Lady will ensure that a guest is safe from harm, but you'll have to be alert with your trading. And keep your dog with you at all times."

My fingers are clammy and sweaty; my stomach is churning. I've been starting to get used to the idea of being the ambassador. I think of how I bargained with the fisher at the farmhouse, and see myself graciously giving and accepting gifts from visitors from our homeland; choosing exquisite things to store, and perhaps to keep — and best of all, being admired and adored, hearing people whisper, "This girl, still a maiden — you see how expertly she trades; how she helps the folk of the Isle of Swallows, how beautifully she dances . . ."

Now those dream whispers are saying, "See that foolish girl? Her father is their land's trading admiral, but she's lost all the goods he left her, cheated at every turn." Bargaining for daily fish is not the same as the complicated balance of trade goods.

"We'll pray to our gods to protect you," Dada says fiercely, pulling me close. "And you'll smile, listen, and trust no one. Keep on singing your mother's spirit; find a goddess you can pray to. Share your worries with Nunu, but only when you're sure no one else can hear."

I hear the finality in his tone; still two more days till the spring festival, but he has prayed and read the signs of the sea, and they must leave at dawn.

The ship is already loaded. Now that we know there are no goods in the palace for me to gift or trade, Dada unloads a giant pithos pot, as tall as my head, packed tight with smaller pots and jugs. They're decorated with the swallows of our clan, made by Nunu's family's workshop. I don't know if Dada chose them for that, but it comforts me.

At the last moment he adds a small bronze dagger. "I paid more than I should have for this, hoping it would trade well when we reach Mycenae," he says. "Use it only if your need is great."

I'm expecting a procession, rituals, and sacrifices when he sails, but in Tarmara he is merely another trader, sailing inauspiciously just before the sailing season begins. We gather in the central courtyard at dawn while the Lady sings the sun to rise, and then walk down to the quay. It is the same procession as when we arrived, with a servant from the palace in place of the wharfman, but this time Mama is walking. It's the first time that she's walked further than the courtyard. Dada holds her arm so that she doesn't wander off, but she isn't wailing.

She starts when Ibi kisses her good-bye and swings onto the ship. She shrieks louder when Dada does the same.

"Quiet!" Nunu says sharply. "You'll call the sea demons, you naughty child!"

Sometimes it works if Nunu speaks to her as if Mama was still a three-year-old and Nunu her nurse. This time it doesn't.

The sailors pick up their oars, and Dada helms out of the channel to the sea and the start of his great journey around the world, all the way to the land of the pyramids where his grandfather came from, back again to our home and eventually, here to us.

Nunu and I take Mama by the arms to lead her back to the palace, while townsfolk, whispering and pointing against evil, stop in the streets to see the wailing woman.

"I am the trade ambassador," I tell myself the next morning. It doesn't feel real.

"I'm on my own," I say, and that does.

"The Isle of Swallows depends on me," I say, and that is terrifying.

As the gray light of dawn filters in the window, I dress. I put on my tunic that ties at the left shoulder, to show that I'm priest-folk; I wear my gold hoop earrings, Pellie's bracelet on my left arm, and my Saffron Maiden's on my right, but no anklets, because I want to look serious, not like a girl preparing for a festival.

The palace-folk are in the courtyard for the dawn ceremony. In our land each household greets the morning with their own gods and in their own home, only going to the temple for the great festivals, but here, with the priest-folk living together in one big tangled family, the Lady is the mother of the house and the only one who can greet the sun. If I'm living here, I have to attend.

I didn't think it would feel so hard to go alone, now Dada and Ibi have left.

How can you represent your land if you can't even go to the dawn ceremony? a voice whispers in my head.

Mama is still asleep, but Nunu is watching me. She waves me off, a flick of her hand saying, *Go, go!*

You can't even get out the door unless your nurse tells you!

127

I'm not going to let that horrible voice defeat me. Calling Chance to my side, I slip out of the room, down the halls, the tiles dew-damp under my bare feet, to the courtyard.

I edge closer to two girls about my age, though I can't tell if they're still in their Learning. Girls here don't shave their heads for the goddess, so their hair is already long by the time they put on women's dress. My short curls feel bare and childish. Maybe that's why the closer I get, the more it feels as if they're not just ignoring me, but gossiping about me. They're leaning in to each other so their shoulders are rubbing and I can tell from the way those shoulders move that they're murmuring secrets and laughter to each other, just the way Pellie and I used to.

If only Pellie were here!

I touch her bracelet. *Pellie, my sister-friend, send me your thoughts!*

A harpy's shriek rips the silence. I want to pretend I can't hear; to pretend it's the Lady entering with a strange new song. But I'm already slipping away, down the halls toward our room, because I know it's Mama. She's woken knowing that Dada and Ibi have gone.

I can't do it. I can't go back into the room to see my mother the way the spirit has abandoned her, screaming as if all the orphans and abandoned lovers in the world were singing their grief out through her mouth. I slip past it down the hall, lurking in shadows until the courtyard empties and the priest-folk are having breakfast — and once again, I should be there, but I can't. My stomach is too tied into knots to face the people who watched me flee the dawn ceremony because of my wailing mother.

Besides, it's my job to trade for my people. It's time to start.

The craft quarter is already busy, clattering with tools and shouts, humming with laughter and song as the artisans bring their work out and set up for the day. I stop in front of the seal-stone carvers with their fine tools for etching complicated scenes on gold and gems, some the size of my baby fingernail, others as long as a finger.

Dada's seal is a ship engraved on a golden agate. He wears it on a thong around his neck — and everywhere in the world, when people see that image stamped onto a clay tablet, they know they can trust the merchandise they're promised.

"You should have your own," Dada said before he left. "I should have thought of it before."

There was no point in reminding him again that I hadn't finished my Learning. "I'll have a swallow flying over Crocus Mountain," I said, and he smiled.

"Order it as soon as you can."

Tomorrow. I'm not ready today.

I move on to the potters. Despite the mounting heat as the kiln is fired, the familiarity is comforting. Apprentices are mixing and kneading clay; one man is starting to roll clay ropes, and the first lumps are being thrown onto wheels. There are three wheels and a potter at each—two women and a man. I watch the way they shape their clay, how they throw and the way they hold, and although the methods are nearly identical, there's something individual in each one.

The pottery waiting to be fired is exquisite, as fine as any of ours, with writhing octopus on fat jars and white flowers on ewers. There are cups and bowls, goblets, jugs, and vases. My fingers itch to touch them.

I smile my praise before remembering that if I'm going to buy I'll need to haggle, and they nod in reply, their hands too wet and busy to salute.

An apprentice is making clay tablets to be taken, still damp, to the scribes for the palace records of goods and taxes. Her hands are fast and sure; it's a lowly task, but I envy her confidence. I wonder if she's worked on the rows of simple clay cups drying in the sun— for the feast tomorrow, I guess, to be used once and destroyed.

"Do you wish to buy?" a woman asks, saluting as she comes out of the storeroom.

"Not today," I say, but as she turns away, something makes me add, "I'll be trading for the Isle of Swallows. I'm the sister of Glaucus—did he buy from you?"

"Glaucus! I can see it now—you have the same nose. I'm not sure I'd say I sold to him—he was that hard a bargainer, it was more like giving it away and being grateful I didn't hand over the kiln as well. No, lass, don't cry—that's just my talk. He was a fair man, and a man who appreciated beauty. I'm sorry for your grief, truly I am."

I didn't know I was crying, but now I can feel tears dripping down my cheeks. I sniff and wipe them off with the back of my hand.

"As for the pots," she says briskly, "he had two great pithoi packed with our best wares—did the captain not find them before he left?"

I shake my head. Her face is kind; I wish I could ask her if Glaucus gambled.

"Perhaps he sold them to another trader first," she suggests.

"Perhaps," I agree.

"When you're ready," she says, "we can do a good deal if you take a big enough shipment. Your brother was a great record-keeper. I don't know what god has stolen my wits this morning, the last thing I need is another trader as shrewd as Glaucus—but you should study his tablets."

"Thank you." *Tablets!* They weren't with his few belongings, the spare cloak and tunic. If it was true that he'd gambled it all away, he might have erased them—but I get the feeling this woman wouldn't believe the gambling story any more than Ibi and Dada did.

"What do I need to offer you for a clay tablet, so I can start making my own records?"

She calls the apprentice, and puts a fresh tablet, smooth and cool, into my hands. "For this one, a smile and a promise to return. The scribes can spare it."

Her kindness starts my tears again. I can't help it and can't stop.

But the potter comes out from her workspace and hugs me; holds me in her strong arms as if I were her own child.

"Life is hard," she says. "But we're all stronger than we think. Even priest-folk."

Drawing back in surprise, I see that she's grinning.

I don't care who sees me; I don't care what the ambassador should do.

I hug her back.

Mama's wailing is down to a hum. Nunu's got her up and walking, round and round the room in circles; she never shrieks as loudly when she's pacing.

"Nunu, when you first set out our things in this room, did you find any record tablets?"

"That's right, child—this ignorant old woman found the trade records and destroyed them without telling the captain!"

"Sorry, Nunu. I just had to check because of what the potter told me."

We both know those records were lost before we arrived. We just don't know if it was before or after Glaucus died.

But if Glaucus hid them, they could still be here.

The only possible hiding place is the carved wooden chest where we keep our clothes and bedding. I take off the lid, kneel and lift our things out.

"What are you doing?" Nunu shrieks. "The chest was empty when we came—I told you I looked."

She's right, of course. There's nothing underneath.

I smooth my hands over the wooden bottom, but it's as solid as it looks, hiding nothing. And it sits flat on the floor, with no room to slip anything underneath.

Flat on the floor, but not flat against the wall. A fancy carved panel has been added to the bottom, running around it like the flounce on a skirt, a good finger's length out from the chest. With the lid off, I can see the gap against the wall.

Even empty, the chest is heavy. I tug so hard I tumble backwards. Chance yelps in fright—and the clay tablets tucked between the chest and the wall crash to the floor.

Only one breaks; I can read them all. Can read the story of Glaucus's trading, what he got for the goods he started with, what he gave as host gifts, what he paid for what he bought: pottery, ten statuettes in bronze, four sealstones . . . He'd traded well, as the potter said, and had rich goods for Dada's next season.

He did not gamble it away. It disappeared after he died.

The trade priest lied. Lied about the dead. Lied about my brother.

Rage bubbles from my belly like a belch from the goddess.

The same angry fire flashes from Nunu's eyes—but Nunu, as she so often reminds me, is old and wise. "We are guests here," she hisses, putting her finger to her lips.

She's right. *Trust no one, Dada said.*

No one can know that we've discovered the trade priest's lie. No one. Even the wise-women Granny and

Wart Nose, who are kind as well as skilled, are part of the palace.

We've been as quiet as we can, but our rage and grief are filling the room and soaking into Mama. Her murmuring crescendoes to a wail.

I shove the chest back into place and slide the tablets into the gap, keeping out the stylus that was hidden with them. Nunu moves quickly, dropping the clothes and bedding inside and replacing the lid. I use it as a seat, and with my brother's stylus and my new clay tablet, start to list everything that Dada has left me.

The first sign, for a dagger, is barely scratched into the damp surface when the wise-women rush in with poppy tea to calm my mother.

Nunu's already singing to her, combing her hair and stroking her forehead. Mama thrashes and shrieks, slapping Nunu's face and throwing the comb to the floor.

"It's the spring festival tomorrow," says Wart Nose. She's kinder than the older one; she talks to Mama as if her spirit is still there, as if she's a person. "Rest today so you can join in."

"Join in?" snaps Granny. "Are you mad? That noise would drown out the Lady's prayers!"

"You won't shriek tomorrow, will you?" Wart Nose says soothingly, manoeuvring Mama onto her bed and encouraging her to drink the calming tea. "You'll sleep now, and your daughter and your nurse will sing your spirit back. Gods and spirits are roaming for the spring; it's time for yours to come home."

So Mama sleeps, and we sing as hard and long as we did right at the beginning in the farmhouse, because it's true that her spirit has been wandering for so long now that we've almost given up trying to sing it back. We still do it every day, but not for long, and sometimes I think about other things while I sing. Today I sing with my heart as well as my voice, and I know that Nunu does too.

Wart Nose is truly kind.

So was the potter. And the Lady.

It's easy to mistrust someone like the trade priest, but trying not to trust these women makes me feel like the earth is moving beneath my feet again. I want Mama back, more than I can bear. Suddenly I'm crying as I sing, the tears that started with the motherly potter turn into great gulping, hiccupping sobs for my real mother, whose spirit is strong and wise, who people trust and respect; who knows what to do.

We sing to her spirit all day and into the long evening, till Nunu's voice cracks and my throat is sore, and still Mama sleeps. But when she wakes in the morning, she doesn't wail. She looks at me and smiles, and says, "Leilei."

My baby name; what I called myself and what Mama and Dada called me till I said I was too old, long before the start of my Learning. I never knew it could sound so beautiful. I kneel by her bed with my arms around her, my head on her shoulder. "Mama, you're back! Your spirit has come home."

"Leilei." She nods, stroking my hair just like she used to, when I was small and needed comfort. "Yes, yes, yes. Fish, fish, fish?"

The words hit my stomach like rocks. Her strong, wise spirit hasn't returned. Maybe it never will.

But some other part of her has, some part of the girl and the maiden and the woman who is Mama, is still there, and that's who knows my name and strokes my hair in the way only my mother can.

As the sun climbs
    I bathe and dress,
    paint face and lips—
    wondering how long my pot
    of saffron will last—
    the embroidered shift first worn
    for the crocus Learning,
    half a year or a lifetime ago,
    and my skirt, in the colors of home,
    its red and black layers
    tied tight at my waist.
Nunu does the same for Mama
    and this time my mother looks
    like a woman with an empty face,
    not a corpse on a bier—
    and I think that empty
    is better than dead.
Nunu, too, is washed and clean
    as even the lowest slaves in the palace
    must be ready

to welcome the season of growing,
    of fertile fields and food for all—
    the fresh new year.
We are ready long before time
    but I cannot wait
    any longer.
In the courtyard,
    in the halls and open rooms,
    the workshops where no work is done
    today,
    a hiss of whispers
    slides around corners
    and between the pillars—
    rules are different here
    if their gods forbid speech on this great day.
    Now my ears are tuning,
    I hear the words,
    catch even the servant talk—
    so harsh and rough it's hardly speech at all—
    and all are of fear,
    omens of darkness
    and wondering what
    the oracle might foretell.
Then someone murmurs—
    a clear priest-folk voice—
    "There's the wailing woman
    who cursed the sea as her husband sailed."
    And my spine tingles
    like hackles on a dog.
But whispers are lost as the sun rises high
    and the courtyard fills:

priest-folk, craft-folk, and town,
flowing into halls and onto roofs
to watch Sarpedon and the Lady
accept from their thrones
tribute from each group:
flowers and honey
grain and dried fish
oil and wine—
a taste of each poured into altar-stone hollows
to feed the gods
and remind our great mother
of what she must produce
if her people are to live and serve.
Now the beasts: two new lambs
and a full-grown goat, rangy and strong.
He fights and bucks,
thrashing even as his dark blood flows
knocking the bowl from the Lady's hands
splashing blood on the Lady and chief.
The gasping crowd moans and mutters
at this most evil of omens—
a sacrifice refusing to be given—
then stills again with shock.
The trade priest leads in a woman—
small and thin as slaves often are,
so young that if she were priest-folk
she might still be Learning—
her hands tied with plaited rope.
She sways beside him as if
she's drunk too much wine
or the wise-women's tea.

"Great Mother," sings the Lady
   "you have sent omens of your rage
   so we offer a gift as never before
   to please your heart."
The woman does not
   struggle like the goat
   or bleat like the lambs
   but lies still where she's laid
   across the bloodied stone
   and the crowd is hushed
   as her life blood drips away
   though I sway and feel I could fall.

Nunu puts a firm hand on my arm. The touch steadies me, but her glare is a clear reminder, *Don't upset the priest-folk—or your mother!* Which is really the same thing, because I don't know what will happen if Mama begins to wail right now.

Luckily, though she understands it's a ritual, standing silently with her hand on her heart, she doesn't seem to have noticed what the last sacrifice was. I step in front of her to block her view as the priests pile flowers and fruit onto the young woman's body before carrying it to the sanctuary.

The Lady and Sarpedon lead the way, the Lady singing a hymn to the goddess,

> *Open your heart, Great Mother,*
> *open your heart as you open the doors*
> *into your underworld dark and drear*

accept this woman with the gifts she bears
into your realm of winter death
and release your daughter,
maiden of spring, bringer of life,
release her into our world
to bring life to our season.

I could almost sing too. Sing with relief that I'm a stranger here and don't have to be in the temple with the other priest-folk and the dead woman. I've seen sheep and goats sacrificed my whole life, but never a person. Even our belchy, bad tempered goddess doesn't ask for that.

People chant the songs of their clans and families as they wait for the Lady to return. They don't dance to call Kora home as we do. *Pellie will be dancing now! Pellie, Rastia, Tullie, and Chella calling the swallows and the Maiden home for spring.* The longing to be with them stabs me, sharp as a knife.

But little Alia, dead long before the spring, won't ever dance again. I fork my fingers against evil, promising the goddess that however long it takes to finish my Learning, I will learn the rites and dance her daughter home.

Nunu paces with Mama; I remember that I've locked Chance in our room, afraid that he might disgrace us during the sacrifices. I let him out and he throws himself against me, yelping with joy. His back is higher than my knees now, but he is still clumsy and doesn't know how big he is. I rub his head and whisper that food is coming, and he stays close as a shadow by my side.

The sun is low before the priests return. Children are restless and fretful from hunger—only babies at the breast will be fed before sunset. But even the toddlers still at the sight of the Lady. Her eyes are glazed in the unmistakeable way of someone who's been talking to the gods.

"Our sacrifices have been accepted. The oracle speaks of great things: a meeting of the gods of sea and air, with gifts we cannot imagine."

The crowd breathes a murmur of relief. The Lady and Sarpedon lead the way out of the courtyard; musicians pick up flutes and rattles, and the folk follow in their clans. Mama joins the procession without being reminded; as honored guests, we walk between the priests carrying buckets of blood, and the craft-folk behind them.

A wide road leads to the barley fields ready for harvest, where the Lady pours blood for the goddess with a prayer for rich crops, and cuts the first stalks with her silver sickle. The path narrows as we reach the olive trees and grapevines, with blood and a prayer in each place.

The sun has set by the time we return to the courtyard. The stacked clay cups I saw yesterday are out in rows. I take one and watch a servant fill it with wine, and, for the first time, wish the dark red didn't look quite so much like blood.

A fire is lit. The flames leap into the darkness, throwing heat and demon shadows. Skewered meat cooks on braziers all around the walls. My mouth waters like a dog's; I didn't know how hungry I was till I smelled it.

More bonfires are lit in the fields and town; we hear bursts of singing and shrieks of laughter, but we stay here, safe in the courtyard with the other priest-folk and the slaves who serve us. And in the feasting, the dancing and singing that go on till the full moon rises, I forget the horrors of the ritual, and think that all will be well.

10

The noise throws us from our beds.

It's too huge to be heard; it bombards us; punching our ears. It's the sound of the end of the world.

In the orange light bursting through the night-time shutters, Mama and Nunu are screaming open-mouthed, hands over their ears. I can't hear them. I'm screaming too, but I can't hear that either.

The air quivers; the earth trembles. My bones have turned to water.

I can't get off the ground.

Get out, get out, get out!

How? Where?

Just out! I'm never going to be trapped in a building again!

Terror forces my legs to obey. I jump to my feet, pulling a tunic over my nightshift; Nunu is doing the same for Mama. I push the door open, fighting against the wind.

A hundred suns are streaking across the darkness, as
if the god of the sea has risen from the depths to juggle
balls of fire. Ashes float in; the earthmother quakes,
and still the noise goes on.

Something knocks my knees and rushes past.
"Chance!"

The puppy ignores my scream and keeps on running.

The oracle was laughing at us. *The gods will meet*,
the Lady said—but they've met in war.

Nunu grabs our bag of jewelry and our cloaks, and
we run to the courtyard.

The sky lit by fire
    as warring gods hurl
    the stars from the sky,
    spears of lightning
    and the shredded sun
    torn from its rest.
The courtyard has no roof to crush us
    but is crowded with panic
    and the thronging chaos
    of people running
    with nowhere to go,
    stumbling over wine-sleeping bodies—
    the lucky ones missing
    the end of the world—
    all of us screaming
    without sound,
    our voices puny against the gods'.
The Lady and priest-women
    flee to the temple;

but I no longer believe
that even the holiest
sanctuary is safe.
And the courtyard crowd,
    herded by terror,
    sweeps us along,
    pushing, shoving—
    no care for class or clan—
    I grab Mama's arm,
    Nunu firm on her other side—
    in all these fears
    the greatest is losing each other—
    and if anyone stumbles
    they'll be trampled to death.
Like a river surging
    we follow in Sarpedon's wake
    down the road to the harbor—
    Sarpedon planning, I think,
    to beseech the sea god
    to make peace with the sky—
    though not even the gods
    could hear against their own roar.
The crowd thinning, spreading
    as it reaches the streets;
    but like the flares through the darkness
    panic sharpens my mind:
    we are ill-omened strangers
    in a crowd that may search for
    another sacrifice tonight.
We drop to the rear,
    watching from the hill

as Sarpedon leads
his priests to the quay.
And the sea,
lit by howling balls of flame
retreats before him.
The water is gone
as if it had never been,
floating ships sink dry on empty sand—
a horror that can't be true,
like the noise too loud to hear.
But Nunu's face—
a mask of fear—
says she's seen the same.
And we turn, pulling Mama with us
the crowd is surging,
some toward the sea
and some away—
but nowhere is safe
a ball of flame torches a house
and a distant hill burns—
we race back to the palace,
barely reaching the courtyard
before the rushing, screaming, trampling crowd
overwhelms us.
But the sky flares stronger;
the sea god spews his wrath,
a wave like a mountain
looming over quays and shipsheds,
swamping storehouses and sailors' homes—
and Sarpedon and his priests
are gone.

In a demon-dream, conjured by gods
    the beached ships
    are on water again
    tossed upside down
    to float through streets
    with the roofs and doors
    of the houses they've smashed.
The murdering wave,
    this mountain of water,
    has reached the gates—
    and we have nowhere
    left to go.
Hollowed by fear,
    my mind floats free
    from my doomed, scared body—
    till rage bursts through it,
    red heat thumping me back into life;
    we've gone through too much
    to be washed away now.
And Chance is too young
    to survive without me—
    I hope he's somewhere high and safe.
But now, like a sigh,
    the wave draws back,
    leaving the houses, the boats and the people
    thrown like scraps to dogs
    across the smashed town.

We're safe for the moment.
    Nowhere is safe.

At least the earth isn't shaking. We'll go back to our room and pack to escape. It doesn't matter where; anywhere is safer than here.

Our door is still open—and the room is still empty. Chance hasn't come back.

But I barely have time to worry about my puppy, because Mama has collapsed onto her bed, and Nunu topples on top of her when she bends to check. She waves me away crossly when I try to pull her up; I hope that means she's all right.

I open the shutters for more light, but my hands are slippery with sweat and shaking so badly I can hardly manage the latch. My chest is tight, and it hurts to breathe. I don't know if that's because I'm panting so hard or because the air is hot, with a strange burning smell that reminds me of the earthmother's belch.

Nunu is saying something. The gods' roaring is just loud like thunder now, not a force hammering against my skin, but I still can't hear.

All I want to do is lie down on my own bed and hope for my puppy to find me when I wake up. Instead I make bundles and fill our baskets the way I did when we fled our ruined home. Nunu tries to get up but can't. I think that was what she was saying.

Suddenly the booming changes, and though I can't see it, I understand. The monstrous wave is coming again. Mama and Nunu can't run, and there's nowhere to go. Not even time to think before the crash as it hits the gates . . . and now water is coming in under the door.

Then it slowly ebbs out, leaving fronds of seaweed on the wet floor and our bundles on the chest untouched. Mama goes to sleep, Nunu frozen in fear beside her. I'm shaking too hard to move.

We have to get out of here! The next wave will get us!

I see them coming, endless, towering, mountains of water till the whole world is covered and there is nothing left.

There's no point in running, but no choice—we have to try.

The next wave comes faster. I'm still trying to sit Mama up when I hear it.

No water comes in under the door. The courtyard, when I sidle out to check, is no damper than our floor. The one after that is lower still, so we stay.

It's two days now, or maybe four. The gods have ended their war, but it's an uneasy peace: ash still falls like rain, and the torn-apart sun never rises. Sometimes there's a strange orange light and sometimes it's the darkest of no-moon nights.

We stay in our room, because I don't know where else to go. I dream of searching for Chance, but the dark is too fearsome and I could not leave Mama and Nunu alone. Nunu and I never sleep at the same time; one of us is always awake, waiting for danger. There is food in the kitchens but no one serving; we scavenge and bring it back to our room, keeping out of people's way. It's not good to be a stranger in a time of fear—and Mama is not the only one wailing now.

The palace, the town, the country are flooded with keening. Sarpedon and most of his priests were swallowed by the sea, along with half the town.

It's time outside time; I can hardly remember when the world was normal, when the sun god rose in the morning and slept at night. Now the Lady doesn't even try to call the dawn.

I wake smelling something that isn't ash from the sky or rot from the sea.

In the kitchen courtyard, in a massive tripod over a flickering fire, a cook stirs a lentil soup thick as porridge. She fills a bowl for me with a nod.

I count the meals in my head as I go down the torch-lit corridor: nine. It's probably only four days, maybe five, since the spring festival.

Suddenly, I realize that the haze is not so dark. I can nearly see across the courtyard, as if it's a smoky room at dusk.

Can it be that the gods have heard our prayers, and the sun will return? And the world we know with it?

How could I even think that? The world will never be the same again.

"A ship! A ship coming in!"

The cry comes up from the town and spreads around the palace. We can tell that it's good news before we hear the words.

Dada! If any captain could survive that wave, and go against the winds to return to this cursed land, it would be him.

We go down to the harbor, Mama, Nunu, and me, with hundreds of other people from the palace and the town. I'm torn between wanting to run all the way because I'm so sure it's Dada, and feeling sick with fear at approaching the sea. But I don't trust the land either: I wrap myself in my cloak and tuck the bag with our jewelry under my arm.

It's the first time we've left the palace since it happened. Now there's light, I'm sure I'll find Chance today too. Dada, Mama, and me, Chance and his mother . . . we'll all be reunited.

But the light shows us more than we want to see. The devastation is worse than any demon-dream could conjure. We stumble into holes on the road where the sea god bit out rocks and spat them into the town. We climb over broken bits of houses and furniture.

I've been thinking that the wave wasn't as bad as our earthquake, because the palace is still standing, but the stink says it worse. The stink of rotting things from the sea that should never be on land. The stink of death. So many people keep washing up that they haven't all been buried yet. Drowned goats and sheep are heaped onto fires to burn, but even the fires stink. I'm afraid to look at them, in case I see my puppy.

We stand on the beach where the quay used to be, by the smashed ships and shipsheds, where the water is thick with floating pumice rocks, and watch the ship come in.

It's not Dada's.

I was so sure! I don't care if no one has ever sailed the wrong way around the trade route before, everything else in the world has changed, so why couldn't this?

Mama obviously thought so too. Her face puckers.

Please don't wail, Mama! Not here, not now!

Nunu hums to her, rocking her gently by the shoulders.

Mama stares imperiously, shrugging off Nunu's comforting hands. "Fish!"

Today *Fish!* means "By the goddess, old woman, what are you doing?"

Nunu catches my eye and grins. While she's angry, Mama won't be wailing.

The ship drops anchor just off the wreckage-littered beach, and the sailors splash ashore. They're speaking a strange language but the captain can speak ours, and an old sailor in the crowd can understand the men. The news filters quickly up from the ship to the watchers.

The murdering wave was no more than a strange swell out at sea. The captain says that the gods waited to hurl it all at the land.

Can that be true? Could it be true for where Dada and Ibi were too?

For an instant there's hope in the world.

But horror is stronger than hope—
two days sail from here
the ship passed the island
where the gods fought over land and sea,
and though gods cannot die
that island has.

The sailors' lungs, far out to sea
    burned in the smoking poison
    steaming out from the land.
    The falling ash, they say,
    was the island's blood
    and the floating rocks its bones.
"You weave like a rock floats,"
    Nunu used to say when I broke my yarn
    because everyone knows
    rocks don't float—
    but now the world has turned
    and they do.
The gray mountain the sailors describe
    is not our island—
    it has no town of white houses
    climbing the hill from the sea,
    no green slopes
    or sheltered harbors—
    but I shiver to think
    that any land could die.
The crowd, too, murmurs and cries
    an uncertain anger at gods in turmoil
    and chieftains gone,
    at land destroyed and tales of worse—
    we are not safe here.
But before I can leave
    I'm drawn to the water's edge,
    wading out to feel, around my ankles,
    the bobbing roughness of rounded rocks—
    because the lumps of gray, red, and black,

though not of our goddess,
are the colors of my land.

Just as seeing the heaps of dead animals made it hard
to believe that Chance has survived, the story of the
smoking island darkens our hope for Dada and Ibi.
We're calling to the goddess from our room—Mama's
"no, no, no!" is as good a prayer as any—when there's a
scrabbling at the door. I open it to a skinny, black, half-
grown dog. He leaps at me; I throw my arms around
him, and we both tumble to the floor.

"Chance! You're alive!"

Tears are streaming down my face, and if dogs could
cry they'd be streaming down Chance's too. He climbs
onto my lap because he can never remember that he's
too big now, and whimpers to tell me how scared
he's been. He's heavy and awkward, and holding him
is the best thing I've ever felt. Nunu clucks at him, and
even Mama smiles.

"You don't need to be afraid now you're with me,"
I comfort him, and though he whines again and hides
his head under my arm, I feel braver too now that
he's back.

Because the palace does not feel safe. It feels like
a hive of bees when the queen has flown. Maybe the
Lady has flown; even now there's enough light to see,
and we can guess that the dawn has arrived, she doesn't
come out to sing the sun—when the sun needs that
song as never before. How can a land survive without
its ritual?

She appears for the first time the next day. She looks pale and sick, dazed with grief. She does not look like a ruler.

The man beside her does. It's the trade priest, the only priest who survived, because he was the only one who didn't go down to the harbor when the great wave came. Now he is Sarpedon, the chief. He feasts the sailors—there are still goats and sheep in the hills to be slaughtered and cooked, though the smell of the grilling meat mingling with the stink of dead animals on bonfires makes me gag.

I eat anyway and gather bones for Chance. Nunu says the servant talk is that the stores of dried food are dwindling fast. The barley in the fields that was ready to harvest has been smothered and scorched. Spring is the season of fresh greens; people should be out picking in the hills, but this year there's nothing to pick. The ash covered it all and the new plants aren't strong enough to push their way through. The gentle spring rains, instead of washing it away, run the ash into pools, where it hardens like rock in the next day's sun.

Worse, any townfolk, fishers, and sailors who survived when their homes and stores were swept away are coming to the palace for food. You don't have to be an oracle to see that only trouble can come from less food and more people.

All my life, I've thought that being Swallow Clan meant we were safe. Not from random cruelties of the gods like illness and accidents, but safe from hunger, from violence and fear.

Now I'm not so sure. I'm not hungry, but I'm afraid it could happen. In fact, I'm afraid all the time. I'm afraid of the crowds of people who come to the palace to demand food, because if Nunu is right, there soon won't be anything to give them. And we have only Sarpedon and a small handful of guards to hold them back.

I'm even more afraid because this Sarpedon doesn't like us. He lied about my brother and he's afraid we know it. No — not afraid: angry. And now he's in power.

He's not the only one who doesn't like us. People point their fingers against evil at our door, and mutter about curses carried from over the sea.

She's my mother! I want to shout. *She was our Lady's sister; she was wise and beautiful and when her spirit comes back she'll be like that again!*

But her spirit isn't back, only a tiny bit of it, and even though she only cries when she hears other people keening, they still don't understand. They remember her wailing as if she was foretelling this disaster, and they hate her.

Most of all, I've been afraid since I saw that slave girl led to the altar. Just like I didn't know priest-folk could go hungry, I didn't know that anyone needed to be afraid of being sacrificed like a goat.

It seems there are more things to be afraid of than I've ever imagined.

The thoughts swirl in my head, as if Pellie and I are arguing:

We need to run away, to find somewhere safe.

We're guests here! Of course we're safe.

Sarpedon hates us.

But this is where Dada will return to.

He won't find us if we're dead like Glaucus. Or like the slave girl.

But where can we go?

That's the one there's no answer to. No answer except to tell Nunu to venture back to the kitchen at different times of the day, to gather extra food, dried figs or fish, barley cakes—things that are light to carry and don't need cooking. At the same time I organize our goods, packing the gold and bronze items into baskets with our clothing.

I'm not quite sure why I'm doing this. It's as if the Pellie part of my brain is planning, and not telling Leira what it's for, because what it's for is too scary to contemplate.

In the end there's no choice. A roar of shouting, of doors being battered, wakes us in the night. There's no time even to dress. We throw our cloaks on over our nightshifts and grab the packed baskets. I peer out of our room; Nunu tells Mama to keep quiet, and for once, she obeys. So does Chance, except for a low, rumbling growl. He hasn't left my side since he returned.

The back gate has been broken down. Men are pouring in, heading for the storerooms. We shelter behind our door till they pass, then run down the corridor and out the shattered gate. It's too dark to see where we're going: "Into the hills!" I whisper, because the sea is no longer safe and neither is the town.

*

We climb steadily upwards. By the time the murky dawn breaks we can look far down to the cemetery where Glaucus lies, and further down to black smoke coiling up from the palace.

Mama is slowing already, and Nunu is panting, but I am thinking like an animal: I can't let them stop till we find an outcrop of rock to shelter against, where no one can take us by surprise from behind.

Nunu pulls a bladder of ale from her basket. I don't ask how she got it—I'm just glad she did, because I'd thought of food but not drink. We each take a sip; Mama wants more and is cross when I stop her. "No, no, no!" she snaps, trying to grab it back from me.

"Fig!" says Nunu, handing her one. "Your favorite!"

Mama chews, and forgets that she's angry. But it takes another one before she forgets that she's hungry.

I don't know how many figs or barley cakes we have, or how long the ale will last, but it doesn't matter—I don't know where we're going or how long it will take to get there. The smoke from the palace is thickening and spreading; we won't be going back to Tarmara.

If townfolk are attacking the palace, it's not safe to be priest-folk.

I hear this as if the goddess herself has spoken in my head, though she doesn't tell me what to do about it. *Don't be Swallow Clan?* It's like saying, "Don't be a girl. Be a dog instead."

I wish I could be a dog. We could follow Chance, scavenge for food, and bite anyone that attacks

us. We wouldn't have to decide if we should go on
walking in our nightshifts or dress properly and tear
our clothes. Our nightshifts are white linen, split at
the sides like our dress shifts, but the front in one piece
that covers our breasts. It's easiest just to wear them.

Trying to remember
    what Dada told me of this land,
    where the best pots come from,
    the bronze and gold
    and where the cities lie—
    Knossos the greatest.
    But Nunu heard the rumor:
    what the sea did to their harbor
    was worse than here
    and riots have smashed the palace.
"Over the mountains to the east," said Dada,
    "barely a full day's sail by sea,
    is Gournia:
    a town of honest traders,
    though smaller than our own—
    I once sat out a five-day storm
    in their wide safe bay."
Perhaps the angry sea
    has spared this town,
    and my heart says,
    "If Gournia sheltered Dada
    it can save us too."
    Dada will be remembered
    and the priest-folk will take us in,

for though we've left the pots behind
　　we still have gold and bronze
　　to trade.
Our ceremonial shifts and skirts,
　　rolled inside our cloaks,
　　are strapped across our backs
　　to keep them clean and whole
　　so when it's safe
　　we can look as priest-folk should.
I find a branch for Nunu to lean on,
　　and we turn to the east,
　　clambering up goat trails
　　with the rising sun in our eyes.
This is not like gathering flowers
　　on Crocus Mountain—
　　the hills aren't higher
　　but go on without end;
　　thorns tear our legs, our arms, and shifts;
　　the smoky sky is dark,
　　lightning flashes without rain—
　　and we won't be returning
　　to hot baths and feasting.
"At least we're not carrying Mama," says Nunu,
　　which is true,
　　though I still wish we had Dada or Ibi
　　and knew how far we must go.
Then Mama starts her *no, no, no* song
　　and I sing with her, but louder,
　　"Yes, yes-yes, yes!"
　　till Nunu laughs, wheezing and coughing.

I think Mama will laugh too—
but she shouts louder,
slaps Nunu, and sits.
I tell her we don't have much food
and no shelter till we reach this town;
we need to keep moving
before the sun is too high to find the east—
but if Mama is sitting we must all do the same
and I can see
that Nunu also needs to rest.
Another sip of ale, a barley cake and fig.
I rub Mama's feet,
wipe blood off her scratched legs
with the edge of my shift.
Chance licks mine,
the only drink he gets.
Smelling bruised thyme
disturbed under ashes
between the rocks where we rest,
I wonder if the goddess will ever
call her plants to return.
We sing to Mama, sing her up to her feet,
over the crest of this ash-covered hill;
a glimpse of the sea where we've come from—
not as far as I hoped
for all the climbing we've done—
down the slope and up one more
to find a safer place to rest
while the sun is high,
our faces shaded and backs guarded.

"Watch while I sleep," I say to Nunu,
    but she is already snoring—
    and so is Chance.
    I'm an almost-woman, young and strong,
    I tell myself
    but after a moment
    I doze too.

We walk on once the sun dips enough that we can be sure of the west. The light is still weak through the haze, and keeping it on our backs is not as easy as walking into it in the morning. The goat trail twists and crooks so we have to keep checking if the glow is still behind us.

When did Nunu get so stiff she can hardly turn her head? She has to pivot her whole body, and now she's so tired that she staggers when she does it. Once, she falls right over.

"Don't look back!" I snap. "I'll take us the right way!"

I need Nunu to be younger. I need Mama to be well. I need Dada to be here.

I need Glaucus to be alive and the world to be right.

In my head, Pellie laughs. *Are you baby, or almost-woman?* she asks, so clearly that I spin around to see her.

She's not there. How could she be? She's safe at home with her mother the Lady and her sister Kora, far from murdering waves and crowds.

I go on walking, and singing to Mama, and turning around to see where the sun is, until I don't need to turn around anymore, because suddenly it's dark. We are not going any further tonight. My stomach cramps in pain.

"Nunu," I whisper, "I think my bleeding is coming early!"

"You're hungry," Nunu says grimly.

I open my mouth to argue, because I've been hungry before—I've fasted from sunrise to sunset on feast days—but I've never felt like this.

Then I remember the sweet barley porridge that Nunu would give me before sunrise on those days. I can almost feel its warmth filling my stomach, and almost cry because it's not real.

"This is the sort of hunger that made my family sell me to your grandparents," says Nunu.

Terror descends with the dark. We're starving in a world the gods have abandoned, without fire or shelter, and a half-grown puppy to protect us.

But as we unwrap our bundles of clothes, I remember the bronze dagger. It's the most valuable thing we have to trade. Hunting dogs are etched along the blade, and a lion's head is carved into the golden hilt—but I don't care about its beauty. It's a weapon.

Tying our flounced woollen skirts over our night-shifts, and our cloaks on top, we huddle together. It's still cold on the rocks, but Chance is warm on my feet, and I clutch the dagger till the handle is hot in my hand and sends strength to my heart.

*

"Sing the dawn," says Nunu.

So I do, because there's nobody else to do it, and even though it doesn't feel right, the sun comes up the way it should, and I think it's a little brighter than yesterday.

Does the Lady sing it in Tarmara today, after the invaders and the fire? What happened in the palace after we fled?

Mama doesn't waste time worrying about things like this. While I am peeing behind a bush, Chance is nosing around further up the hill, and Nunu is bundling our skirts and cloaks, Mama grabs the drink skin and gulps the rest of the ale.

We finished the barley cakes last night. There are six figs left; Mama cries when I say we have to leave three of them so we can have something later.

"They'll taste better when we've walked a little way," I tell her—but one fig or two, we'll still be hungry, and most importantly, we'll still be thirsty.

These mountains had snow on their peaks before the ash covered everything. If we keep on walking, we're bound to find a river—or even a little creek— just a trickle of snow melt will make us happy.

We step into the creek before we know
    and the thick ash sludge
    is up to our knees,
    as if a hearth has been washed
    before the embers are cleared.

Sandals slide and slip from our feet—
　　I reach and search
　　till all my shift is as mud as the hem—
　　I find three sandals
　　but never the fourth
　　and think Nunu is lucky
　　to have never known shoes,
　　though her old legs are trembling
　　with pushing through muck.
Mama feels the wetness; scoops it up,
　　choking as ash smears black
　　across her lips.
　　"No!" I snap,
　　but the thirst wins,
　　and Nunu and I try it too,
　　spitting grit between our teeth,
　　harsh moisture on our tongues.
　　Only Chance doesn't care.
Shivering out to the other side
　　my wet shift clinging, foul with ash,
　　Mama's wet only to her knees,
　　though she slaps at it, "No, no, no!"
　　as if it could learn to behave.
Nunu pulls off her tunic—
　　thorn-shredded up the side—
　　rubs Mama's legs with the drier part,
　　dresses her in formal flounced skirt
　　then helps me do the same.
　　But no gossamer shift to tear on thorns—
　　till our nightshifts dry
　　we'll go bare-topped as farmers.

Not far from the mire
　　that was once a stream
　　we find another path;
　　skirts catching prickles and thorns;
　　my right foot, bare on the stones—
　　I've given Mama my sandal—
　　bruised and bleeding
　　like the wounded Kora.
　　I think of how she bears her pain
　　and maybe I can too.
I don't care where the path goes
　　but it may lead us to help
　　because the cruel fact is
　　we can't do this alone.
　　And at worst
　　it's still leading us east
　　through the spiny forest.
At siesta time, when the sun is high
　　we eat our last figs—
　　our throats so parched we can hardly swallow—
　　and rest in tree-shade,
　　Mama and Nunu dozing,
　　open-mouthed and twitching.
I clutch my dagger
　　because demons were howling in the night
　　and some of them
　　might have been wolves.
　　I only know wolves
　　from stories and furs—
　　but I know that Chance
　　isn't big enough to fight them.

We need to find people—
    if we're not the last alive in this world—
    and shelter and food.
    I pack our empty baskets
    one into the other
    and find two strong branches—
    a crutch for each, Mama and Nunu,
    then wake them from their rest.
Mama is cross, throws her crutch away—
    though when I use it,
    easing the pain in my wounded foot,
    she takes it back.
Trudging, stumbling,
    we limp on through the day,
    eagles circling above—
    wishing my spirit could soar with them
    spying out what lies ahead
    and what we've left behind.
The sun is lowering—
    I don't know how we can face
    another night of fear and hunger—
    when Chance growls
    and we hear the bleating of goats.
    I see a flock below us,
    and a lone boy building a fire
    by a shelter of rocks and branches.
His dog standing alert,
    hackles raised, growling to see us
    and starting to charge;
    the boy shouts him back,

his hand on its shoulder,
    like mine on Chance.
"Greetings, strangers,"
    he calls, a quaver in his voice,
    "are you tree-spirits,
    or women abandoned by the gods
    to wander lost in the hills?"
Abandoned by the gods
    is exactly how I feel
    though it seems a dangerous reply.
    I can't think
    how to explain why we're here—
    faces blackened with mud,
    bare as peasants though in elegant skirts,
    gold on throats and arms,
    not clad in goatskins
    as his mother and sisters must be.
    And though Nunu's gray hair is plaited tight
    and my curls too short to tangle,
    my ponytail is a knot
    and Mama's hair a nest of snakes.
But before anyone speaks,
    Nunu moans and drops to the ground.
"Old mother!" shouts the boy,
    rushing to her as Mama shouts "No!"
    and I kneel by her side.
Nunu's eyes flutter and she tries to rise
    but the boy lifts her,
    carrying her to the fire
    and pulling a goat fleece from the shelter.

168

"Lay this under your grandmother
    when I lift her."
Mama weeps hot tears—
    the goatherd thinks it's for Nunu's frailty
    not for being mistaken
    as her daughter—
    this is not the moment to explain.
From a skin bag
    the boy squeezes milk into Nunu's mouth,
    offers to Mama, then to me.
    The milk is sour, creamy and thick
    smooth on my throat,
    rich on my tongue
    like a gift from the gods.
"You've come far?" the boy asks,
    though he knows we have—
    it's easy to see we don't belong.
    "You must eat and rest
    till the old one is well."
He doesn't ask more
    but tells what he's seen
    since the gods burned the sky:
    people fleeing the angry sea,
    drowned houses and hunger.
    He's brought his flock up high,
    searching—not finding—
    new grass and clean water
    but has heard news from the shore.
"Some folk blame the priests.
    Priest-folk take our first fruits,
    tax flocks, and harvest to please the gods.

Now the gods have destroyed the world—
the priests have failed;
and we don't know why
we've obeyed them so long,
storing food in their palace
and going hungry ourselves."
"No, no, no," says Mama,
which is as wise
as anything I could say,
and the boy, watching us, adds,
"But I say the priest-folk
must live as they can,
and even in lean times
a goatherd needn't go hungry."

Chance stays tucked behind my skirt, nervous of the goatherd's dog, who growls every time Chance pokes his head out. The boy smiles. "Smart pup. My dog wants him to know who's boss."

He whistles, and as he drags prickly branches into a rough fence around the shelter, his dog rounds up the herd. Chance watches and joins in, yipping and darting at reluctant strays till they are all in the corral: billy goats, nanny goats, and a few early kids. The goatherd drags a last branch across the opening. The dog sniffs Chance, who rolls onto his back, offering his defenseless belly.

"They'll be all right now," says the goatherd.

Talking gently to the goats, he moves around them, stroking heads, feeling udders and bellies. When one kid has finished drinking from its mother, the boy pulls a wooden bowl from a thong around his neck, squats at the nanny's side and milks it into the bowl. He pours the milk into a skin bag like the one we drank from, "for yogurt," he explains, and goes on checking the goats.

I don't know how he can tell them apart. They all look the same to me, but he talks to them as if they can understand, moving slowly through the flock till he's checked each one. He milks another nanny and adds the milk to the same bag.

"Most years she'd fill this bag herself," he says sadly, and more sadly still, comes to a small kid nuzzling hopefully at its thin mother. He calms the mother with words I can't hear before carrying the kid away, stroking it and singing what sounds like a prayer.

Squatting again, he holds the wooden bowl between his knees as if he's milking, still stroking the kid. Then his hand flashes; I see the gray flint blade and the redness gushing from the little goat's opened throat.

The mother goat bleats once and he calls to her, soothing, even as he skins her kid and prepares it for the fire.

"This mother is old," he says, seeing me watching. "She couldn't find enough grass under the ash to make milk. The kid would have died of hunger in the coming days. So it gives its life for its mother and for us: now she has a chance of staying alive another year. And we will eat well tonight."

The bones and smoke are offered to the gods as ceremoniously as any priest would do it. The bowl of blood is set on a rock by the fire, and the meat threaded onto green branches to cook.

I'm learning a whole story here, in a way I've never seen it before: the hungry kid, the bleating mother, and me, the end of the story, with my mouth watering at the smell of roasting meat. It seems you can feel sorry and hungry and grateful all at the same time.

And I am very grateful. Nunu has revived with the milk and the rest; we eat hot roasted flesh and sleep near the fire with our faces greasy and our bellies full. The goats and their herder will be moving higher into the mountains tomorrow; we can't stay with them but we'll leave stronger. And wiser.

"What is your plan?" the boy asks next morning, when we have shared the blood pudding that set in the night and washed it down with milk from the same bowl.

I hesitate, but there seems no reason not to tell him where we're headed. "We hope to find work at the palace in Gournia." I stumble over the "work"—it's help we need.

"It would be safer if you weren't so obviously priest-folk. Better if you looked more like servants who fled when your homes and workshops were drowned."

"But we weren't wearing our shifts!" I blush—it's humiliating to have arrived with my shoulders bare, though my nightshift is covering them now. "And we're so dirty—how did you know?"

He laughs. "Your skin is soft under the dirt. Your mother wears sandals; your feet are bleeding as if they've never gone barefoot. And your jewelry is gold."

"We could be goldsmiths."

"Goldsmiths' hands are hard and scarred, and they're smart enough not to wear their art. People are scared and hungry; you don't know what they'll do." He shudders, and I wonder if finding fresh grass for his goats is the only reason he's come so high up the hills. "At least hide your gold. You could perhaps be palace servants who fled when their masters were killed—but a servant wearing gold looks like a thief."

"We're not thieves!"

"I know." He smiles.

Like a swallow changing flight, the hot rage at his accusation turns to scald me. *Now I need a goatherd to tell me how to behave?*

"Thank you," I say, saluting with my hand on my heart as if he were an equal.

Maybe he is!

A strange thought.

The goatherd doesn't want to accept a host gift, but he's helped us in more ways than the food, and I'm grateful. I give him the small gold earrings that have been mine since childhood. I'm still wearing the bigger hoops Mama gave me on crocus-gathering day—I can't give away part of my sacred Learning.

"While we're walking," I decide, "the jewelry is safer being worn than in a basket. We'll take it off and hide it before we reach people."

But I loop Mama's dragonfly necklace around my waist, tucking it securely out of sight under my wrapped skirt, with the dagger belted tight at my hip. Nunu wears three of Mama's bracelets—that will be quicker than taking them off Mama in an emergency.

The goatherd half-fills our ale bag with milk and puts a piece of last night's roasted meat in my basket, covering it with leaves to keep the flies away.

"Follow this path till the sun is high," he says. "Walk with care after siesta; where the path forks, one leg goes to the sea and the other to a small settlement. The settlement folk believe the gods died on that night—it is not a good place."

"We'll head toward the sea," I promise.

We're partway down the hill before it strikes me that even after all the discussion, he saluted us like priest-folk to say good-bye.

11

The bandits strike before we reach the fork in the path.

We'd stopped when the sun was high, drunk some of the souring milk and eaten half the meat. The day was cool enough that Nunu and I were still wearing our cloaks, but Mama insisted on wearing the fine fishnet shawl instead. Then she didn't like the way I'd rolled her cloak to tie around my shoulders, and took it back, draping it on top of the shawl. I knew she'd be too hot but it was easier not to argue.

Our ceremonial shifts were fine enough to pack into one basket, but before going on, we'd picked more leaves and nestled the jewelry into the other one, under the remains of the meat. I hated taking Pellie's bracelet off, and my earrings, but being accused as a thief would be worse.

"Glad to get rid of them," Nunu said, rubbing her bony wrists as she pulled off Mama's gold. "Don't feel right!"

It doesn't make any difference; it all happens so fast. I'm in the lead on the narrow goatpath, Chance at my side, Mama behind me, and Nunu with her crutch at the rear. Mama's lost her stick again and I haven't stopped to cut her a new one.

A demon roar; men dressed in rough skins are grabbing me, ripping my basket away, yanking my arm nearly out of the shoulder. Chance growls, springs and yelps; there's a punch to my ribs before I can scream, and I'm sprawled across the rocks, pain shooting down my hip.

The men rush on, still shouting, and now Mama is screaming, spinning off balance as they rip the cloak from her shoulders and shove her away, and I can't breathe because she's landed on top of me, hard and heavy. Chance is beside me, whimpering.

Nunu hits the last man with her stick but he just laughs, grabs the ale bag and keeps running.

Two men, three, four? It was all so fast I don't even know.

"No, no, no," Mama moans, trying to sit up, squeezing air out of me with every move. I gasp, and she realizes she's lying on me. For an instant it jolts her back into herself. She scrambles off me, onto her knees, kissing my forehead. "Leilei," she moans, "no, no, no?"

I've landed on my right side; pain tingles from my right wrist up to my shoulder and down from my left yanked-out shoulder to my fingers, but what frightens me is the deep throbbing pain from my right hip and thigh. I have landed on the dagger.

How long does it take to bleed to death?

I didn't even use it—and it's killed me.

Stupid, stupid.

How will Mama and Nunu survive without me?

I can't die! I won't. Goddess help me, this is not my time.

Very carefully, I roll from my side to my back. Mama is still leaning over me. Chance has stopped whimpering and is licking my foot. Nunu is moaning, kneeling on all fours. I watch them as if they are a distant painting, and touch my hip. Finger the torn fabric of my skirt, feel my bare skin beneath. It hurts to touch.

Hurts . . . but my fingers aren't wet. No blood—the skin is whole. I've landed on the flat side of the blade; I'm bruised, not wounded. I'm not going to die.

"Goddess leaping," breathes Nunu, crawling over to check Mama and me. "Those slime-eating sons of demons—I thought he'd killed you with that punch."

"So did I," I say. "Can you stand?"

"In a minute," says Nunu.

I start shaking then, so hard that my teeth chatter. Mama strokes my forehead till it stops. Then, slowly, carefully, we help each other to our feet. I find Nunu's stick where the bandit threw it. We check the ground in case something small, an earring maybe, has fallen from the baskets, but we'd packed them too well. All our gold is nestled in the leaves, waiting for the bandits to find when they've eaten our meat.

Maybe they only wanted the meat. Food, and whatever drink was in the nearly empty ale bag. They might not even notice the jewelry.

I hope they never find it! Better for it to be lost in ashes and dirt!

I don't want those horrible men—those slime-eating sons of demons—to touch the Saffron Maiden's beautiful earrings and bracelet that were my grandmother's grandmother's and then mine; I don't want them to shove Pellie's bracelet onto their wrists; I don't want them to see our embroidered shifts. I want to throw up when I think of our gold in their filthy hands.

What I want doesn't make any difference. Our food, jewelry, ceremonial shifts, and Mama's cloak are gone. The clothes we're wearing, the two warm cloaks and the light net shawl, the necklace hidden around my waist, and the dagger: these are all we have left.

We keep on walking. Just before the fork we see the settlement the goatherd warned us about. A skin-clad figure is in front of one of the huts, and even Mama understands that we have to go as quickly and quietly as we can.

We keep tight together, walking crouched and nearly holding our breath, till we're out of sight on the path to the sea.

Even then we don't feel safe. I don't think I'll ever feel safe again. *That man, that demon-bandit hit me! Punched me, on purpose, as if I were a slave. A nothing.*

No one has ever hit me before. I didn't know it could happen. The pain in my ribs reminds me with every breath; the pain in my leg reminds me on every step.

And the pain in my stomach reminds me that we have no food.

Ahead of us is a creek: thick with ashes like the first one, but still flowing. Chance laps at it and we follow, scooping water with our hands. We rest there with our sore feet cooling in the stream until lying on the ground hurts more than standing up.

We have nothing to carry water in, so I hate to leave the creek. But I don't know where it goes, and we need to find a palace where there are priest-folk, people like us, who will take us in and help. So we drink as much as we can hold, filling our bellies full to bursting, and follow the path. We don't get far before we have to stop to pee.

The sky is still murky, making it hard to tell when night is falling. It seems so long since the bandits hit us that I'm starting to believe we've walked through an afternoon and a night without noticing.

Now it's suddenly, definitely, night; a blackness of no stars or moon, and we're still on the path. After trying to be invisible all day, now I long to see a friendly fire.

There is no friendly fire; no food, warmth, or shelter. We lie down where we are, and I am as stiff as an old woman in the morning, aching and limping like Nunu; Mama could be the youngest, though even she moves more slowly than usual. Chance moves hesitantly, as if his ribs are as sore as mine. Nunu thinks the yelp I heard was the bandit kicking him.

But once he's stretched and yawned with the rest of us, he feels well enough to briefly disappear and return stinking like a dead goat. Which is probably exactly what he's eaten and rolled in. He's so pleased with himself that he can't understand why we don't want him to rub against us.

I sing the welcome to the sun as it begins to rise, though my voice is no stronger than its brightness. Then we go on walking.

It's late in the afternoon before we come to another settlement, a cluster of farmhouses and buildings. There are no choices now. My stiffness is easing, but Nunu is stumbling and has fallen twice. And Mama hasn't stopped her low *no, no, no* chant since she woke.

"Hush, Mama," I tell her. "Singing will make you even thirstier."

She looks at me as if I'm speaking a strange language. "No, no, NO!" And she goes on singing.

I step back out of sight. Undoing the sash of my skirt, I slip Mama's necklace from around my waist, and wiggle the silver dragonfly off the chain. Nunu helps me fasten the necklace around my waist again and tie my skirt securely on top. The dragonfly stays hidden in my hand.

"We need something to trade," I say to Nunu's look, and she nods.

The farmers here are not as welcoming as the goatherd, but they are not bandits. They line up suspiciously as we approach, shooing children behind their mothers, as if we might eat them.

One woman stands in front, flanked by men holding clubs. I approach cautiously and salute. The goatherd convinced me that we should stay as close as possible to the truth without admitting to our clan.

"We have run from the riots in Tarmara," I tell her, and hand her the silver dragonfly. "I offer this emblem of the goddess, in honor of her guiding us to you in our quest for shelter."

She takes it with a slight, suspicious smile that turns to wonder as she studies it. The dragonfly is surely the finest thing she's ever held.

The men relax their grips on their clubs; some wander off to continue what they were doing before we appeared. "We don't shelter runaway slaves or thieves," says the woman. "But we will honor the goddess by offering you food and shelter for the night."

Runaway slaves or thieves? How dare she!

Nunu glares at me. "We thank you," she says, and I swallow my hot words.

We sleep on the floor of the main room. "They don't trust us near the stores," Nunu whispers.

That's probably smart. How much hungrier would we have to be before I would steal to stay alive?

But we're not hungry now; we're not cold and the door is closed against wild beasts. My dagger is tucked into my waistband, though I sleep so soundly that when a young boy shouts that it's sunrise, for a moment I don't know where I am.

My leg doesn't know either. It throbs with pain from hip to knee and I don't know if I can walk to leave.

But I can, of course I can. The family sings the dawn—all of them, the whole community out in front of the buildings in the gray light, singing as one, staring at us until we join in too. It's not the same as our song but the tune is simple and the words easy to follow, even in this rough dialect. It's a strange way to do it, but the sun rises so quickly that it seems it approves. It might even be glowing a little more brightly again.

They share their breakfast porridge with us, the barley warm and filling in our bellies, and point us on the path to Gournia. We'll be there by nightfall, they say.

"Which nightfall?" Nunu grumbles.

But I'm excited. I can't help it. The pain in my hip and leg is easing as I warm up. And the haze definitely isn't as thick today—we can already see further over the hills than we could yesterday. *We'll see the sea again soon.* I feel anxious not seeing that blue. It's not natural to have land on every side.

Even Nunu cheers up as we walk. Mama hums a cheerful *no, no, no* song, and when we come around a bend and look out at a grayness that is definitely the sea, I sing praise to the goddess. She answers by showing us a tree to rest under at noon—and before nightfall, just as the farm woman said, we see the stone walls of a town. Houses and workshops stretch down to the sea, and a tall building in the middle must be the palace of the priest-folk.

As the sun sets, we hear a chorus of chirping, and the hazy red sky fills with birds, swooping and darting: swallows. The sign of our home, of spring and rebirth.

We will be safe now.

12

Men armed with clubs and scythes patrol the outskirts of the town. They let us through to the gate, where the captain has a dagger and breath like a dog's.

"No one enters after dusk—get back to the camp!" he orders, pointing at a smelly, noisy confusion of people on the west of the town, small campfires the only sign of comfort.

But finally, it's safe to tell the truth. My shoulders sag with relief.

"We're women of the Swallow Clan—kin to your priest-folk."

"Welcome!" he'll say, apologizing for his confusion and sending a runner to prepare for us. To prepare food, a drink, and a bath before we're presented . . .

Dogbreath looks at us and laughs. "I don't know what it's like where you come from, but our leaders don't wander around like lost goats in the night. It's the camp for the likes of you—and they'll be glad to see you've brought your own dinner."

He means Chance! No one's going to eat my dog!

The guard stops laughing and waves us away with his dagger. "I don't care where you sleep, but no one gets into the town tonight, and no strangers get into the palace until day and night are as they should be. Our Lady and her clan are working to appease the moon goddess and her brother the sun. They have no time for visitors or beggars. If you want help, go back where you came from. We have enough trouble of our own."

It's like being punched in the stomach. Thoughts whirl in my head, and I can't breathe.

Where else can we go?

But I saw the swallows! They were an omen.

What are we going to do?

Mama's face crumples. She doesn't have to understand all the words to feel their meaning from gesture and tone. Nunu's face is blank, but her body looks as if it's shrunk. She's only as big as a ten-year-old child at her fiercest—if she gets any smaller she'll disappear.

So it's not *what are we going to do?* It's *what am I going to do?*

What am I going to do? What am I going to do? What am I going to do?

Have I said it out loud? Does it matter if I have? No one cares.

I take Mama's hand. "Come. We'll find somewhere safe for the night."

"She won't like the camp," Nunu mutters.

"We're not going there!" Not even if eating Chance was a joke. We can hear the sounds of too many people in too small a space: babies wailing, adults shouting in anger or frustration. Too much noise for Mama to bear—and her screeching might be too much for everyone else. We would not be safe.

I turn as if I know where I'm going—as if there is somewhere to go when it's nearly dark and we've been turned away from the town we've been walking to for five days. The place we've lost everything to get to.

There's a tap on my shoulder. I jump, shudder—and reach for the dagger tucked into my skirt. Nobody is ever going to beat and rob me again.

It's one of the young guards; he has a stick, but uses it only to point in different directions. "The purple works are over to the right of the bay—your nose will tell you soon enough if you get too close. The fisherfolk live on the left side; they've lost everything, but they won't bother you if you camp close by."

The words filter through slowly—this is the best we can hope for.

He's being kind, even though he's not supposed to.

So I salute him as an equal, just like I did the goatherd. And just like the goatherd's, his face is kind.

He's better looking, though.

We walk toward the left of the bay, quick as we can because it will be dark soon, though we're twice as slow as when we still had hope.

The purple works smell just like the purple village at home—turning the other way is easy. We bypass the small fires of the fisher-folk who've lost everything, and find a rock wall, a ruin from the days when giants lived on the land; it's close enough to the sea that we can hear the waves shushing below us, but too high on the cliff for them to come up to drown us.

In the corner of broken walls
    built when the gods were young,
    we huddle under cloaks—
    Mama in the middle for warmth,
    and to make sure she doesn't wander—
    but even with Chance at my side
    I am more alone,
    colder than I've ever been
    because I was searching for safety
    and I failed.
I am not good enough
    to save my Mama,
    to help my homeland
    or even myself.
    I will never get home,
    never finish my Learning
    or become a woman.
But in the morning
    the sun rises, though my song is weak—
    I don't know the custom here
    or who is listening,
    I just know the dawn needs
    all the help she can get—
    and when I finish

the sun glows stronger
and so do I.
The guard last night was confused
because of our filth.
We will wash in the sea;
Nunu will do our hair as best she can
and I will offer a gift
that will buy us shelter.
The sea is cold and salt;
we have no oil to smooth our skin
or kohl or rouge to paint it,
not a grain of saffron,
but Nunu's fingers are wise,
combing out Mama's thick plait
and my thin tail in its fuzz of curls.
And though our tops are nightshifts,
filthy from hem to neck,
she tucks them so smooth
and ties our skirts so straight,
no one could possibly think
we were runaway slaves.
Mama's golden chain
is around her neck where it belongs
and the bronze dagger
is back at my waist.
The guard at the gate
is older than Dogbreath
and his face is kinder.
Hope rises as I tell him,
"I am Leira of the Isle of Swallows,
daughter of Lally,

whose speech was lost
when the gods shook the earth.
My father the captain
left me in good faith at Tarmara
to care for our land's trade
but he told us of your great town,
and when we fled the riots and the sea
we remembered his words—
though bandits robbed us on our way."
The guard's eyes widen,
his face pales in shock—
though he must have heard
of riots and bandits before—
so I rush on before he can speak,
and hand him my dagger,
gold hilt first.
"We carry this gift to your goddess
and ask sanctuary of your Lady and chief
as priest-folk kin."
I have never heard
a guard whisper before,
taking the dagger
with a muttered, "Wait here,"
as if his speech is as lost as Mama's.
We wait so long—
standing straight though bellies rumble—
that the sun's shadow leaves the gate.
But the guard, when he returns,
moves slowly
and his eyes do not meet mine.

"The Lady has offered your gift;
        the goddess has spoken.
        The land you name,
        where the gods of sky and sea
        fought the earth's great mother,
        is no more.
"The ashes of its death
        are blighting our land
        just as its wave
        destroyed homes and ships—
        its name will not be spoken
        and all who come from it
        are cursed."
"No!" shrieks Mama,
        or maybe it's me.
    Suddenly my mind hears
        Dada's voice saying the oracle
        proclaimed worse death to come,
        warning him to sail
        before the season had begun—
        but it still can't make this true
        and I struggle to hear the guard:
"The chief says you may stay in the camp
        with the other homeless,
        and find work as you can.
        You may enter the town in daylight
        to collect water from the well,
        but rations for this day only.
"And in the camp or outside
        he warns you to never

mention your homeland again
or claim to be priest-folk or kin."

My tongue has stuck to the roof of my mouth. My throat is so dry it clicks. *I've lost my speech, just like Mama!*

And what is there to say? There are no lessons in courtesy for being told to deny who you are.

"Andras!" shouts the guard, and the boy who showed us the way last night comes running—I don't know from where because my mind is so black that I'm seeing through layers of veils. "Take them to the storerooms and see that they're given a day's rations."

Andras nods; beckons for us to follow, and we do, obedient as slaves—*are we slaves now, if no longer priest-folk?* Is this what Nunu thought, when she was sold to my grandparents?

Slaves get fed. That thought is important. I'm very hungry. Half of me is disgusted with the hungry half. The hungry part says it wants to survive.

Out of sight of the old guard, Andras asks, "Last night I wasn't sure—I didn't really think you were runaway servants—but you're priest-folk!"

"Not if we want our rations!" snaps Nunu, and Andras laughs, because a blind dog could see that Nunu is not a priest-woman.

"I thought that the chief might allow lost priest-folk in, once it was daylight."

"He's ordered that we mustn't claim to be who we are," I say bitterly, "or ever mention where we come from."

Andras's fingers flash against evil.

Why am I so stupid? I've just told him exactly what I've been ordered not to. And we need those rations!

"Goddess weeping!" he breathes. "I knew you were alone—but you're the last of your people!"

"There are as many islands in the sea as there are meanings to an oracle!" I snap. "The land the sailors saw dying was not our home."

He nods, half convinced.

"Our island and its people are strong. My father and brother will return from the trading season with goods to rebuild, and we'll see it again next year."

How will they find us? I've got nearly a year to work that out. Right now we need food.

The storeroom is packed tight with pithoi, rows and rows of huge pots—but the room itself is not huge, and when Andras asks for the rations, the woman asks him to help her lay one of the pots down so she can reach in for the last dried fish. "All those are already empty," she says, pointing.

There are two small dried fish for each of us, a handful of chickpeas and another of barley.

"Homeless rations," says Andras. "They have nothing to cook with."

The woman raises her eyebrows in surprise but says nothing. She exchanges the barley for a small stack of barley cakes.

"Do you have a jug for ale?" she demands.

"No."

"Or a wineskin?"

"No." *We have nothing.* It sounds too pathetic—I can't say it.

The storekeeper stares at the gold around Mama's neck. Does she think we're going to offer her that for a jug of ale?

"Wait!" says Andras, and disappears. Time stands still while he's away; the woman is studying us with open, hostile curiosity, Nunu is glaring her down, Mama is crooning "no, no, no," Chance is licking an oil spot on the floor, and I—I don't really know what I'm doing. I'm floating somewhere outside my body, watching all this and the pale, worried girl that is me.

Andras returns with a clay jug, too misshapen to be an accurate measure.

"My cousin Teesha is the potter's apprentice," he says, as if that explains it. "She was supposed to smash it—but she gave it to me."

He's looking at me as though I should say something, but my mind is still struggling to think through its veils. *This is the ugliest jug I've ever seen.* No, that's not right. *I made better ones as a child at Nunu's knee.* Not that either.

"For you—she gave it to me for you. So you can get your ale today, and water from the well." He hands the jug to the storekeeper, who fills it from a barrel at the end of the room and gives it back to me.

Idiot! It's a gift! It doesn't matter what it looks like—it's a jug, and it's yours.

"Thank you," I say at last, hand on heart, my face glowing hot as a sunburned boy's. I hope he couldn't guess what I was thinking. "Please tell your cousin we are grateful and beseech the gods to reward her kindness."

We move out of the storeroom with its suspicious keeper into a quiet corner of the square. Andras is still with us, and he's blushing too; I don't know why.

But there are other more important things I don't know: where we go now, where we can live, what we'll eat tomorrow, what the guard meant by finding work . . .

Nunu is quicker than me. "Young master," she interrupts the silence, "you have given us time and help, and I offer you a grandmother's blessing. But we are strangers, and do not know what the guard meant by work that we might find. I have raised two generations of children—are there households that need help in this way?"

Andras shakes his head. "Since the war of the gods, every house is full with family who have lost their homes; there are more willing servants than people to serve—and the folk who can afford them still have their slaves. Folk might be grateful for a child nurse in these hungry times, but they'd have no room to keep you, let alone the priest-woman and the maiden."

"You can't call us that!"

"Sorry," he says, blushing again. "But that's the other problem. Everyone will know that you're priest-folk— so if the palace doesn't trust you, they won't either."

"Like the storekeeper?" I ask. It still takes me by surprise when people don't try to please me. In Tarmara I thought it was because of Mama's wailing, but she's not shrieking now. This is just because of who we are.

Panic rises in my throat; I want to claw out of my own skin till I become invisible.

"She doesn't know how to talk to people who look like priest-women and need help like beggars," Andras confirms.

"So why don't you mind?" The words come out before I think. I haven't had a conversation with a boy my age since I started my Learning—until the goatherd, and now this boy, Andras. Does it count if they're not our clan? I don't know the rules anymore.

He doesn't either. Maybe these rules have changed, like everything else. "My family are seal-stone carvers. Priest-folk like to discuss their seals—the stone, the design—with the person making them. I've learned that we're not so different."

"I can say that we're craft-folk! I can spin . . ."

"Like every other child in the world," sniffs Nunu.

"And weave."

"There's a weaving workshop for trade, for the fabric to be dyed at the purple works," Andras explains, "but most of their wool was lost in the flood, so they have nothing to weave now till the sheep can be shorn again."

I can find the flowers the goddess requires in different seasons, the lilies, anemones, and crocuses; I can pluck saffron threads and dry them for make-up and medicine; I can sing and dance in her praise. But those are all the things I'm not allowed to do here.

"If you go to the homeless camp, you'll be sent to labor wherever the palace needs you, and be paid in rations."

"Not the camp!" I protest.

"Or you might be able to work with the fishers. They've lost homes and boats; they might feed you in exchange for help with their rebuilding."

Hope flashes through me again. "I know about boats! My father . . ."

"If the chief said . . . I wouldn't mention your father's ships."

He's right. We're not Swallow Clan. Dada isn't an admiral or a captain. We're nothing and we come from nowhere.

"Andras!" shouts the guard at the gate.

"I thought you were a seal-stone apprentice?"

"That's for normal times. Until the troubles are over, every man and boy has to take his turn at guard duty."

Normal times. I can hardly remember what that means.

"Good luck!" Andras calls, and races away. Mama waves like a child; Nunu and I look at each other.

"A barley cake each and our ale," I say, "then we'll find the fishers."

Every crumb and drop is gone, and I'm still not ready. A feast wouldn't have been long enough.

Don't think about feasts! Don't think about creamy cheeses and roasted snails and figs and goat skewers and honey cakes and . . .

"We're servants," I say. "Mama and I are a priest-woman's maids, from a place where the maids dress like their mistresses. The master was a sea captain, and we fled when the house and its people were taken by the sea."

Nunu nods. "Where is this town?"

"On the other side of Tarmara. It's not a town, just a settlement that we won't name because it was taken by the gods."

"They made pots there," Nunu says sadly.

"Beautiful pots," I agree. "Painted with the sign of a swallow. But they're all gone."

Last night it was too dark to see the beach and the houses near it; this morning we walked on the cliff path and I'd been thinking too hard to look around me.

Now I'm looking. Now I understand why they have guards at the gates; why they give only one day's rations to the homeless; why everyone is scared. It's not that it's so different to what we saw at Tarmara, but some horrors are fresh every time you see them.

From the beach to the center of the town, the ground is littered with wreckage—fragments of houses, pieces of boats, bits of I don't know what. And it's not just wood: stones have been rolled away from walls, tossed onto other walls. Chunks of pumice are scattered on top of everything else, with sand, dead fish, and seaweed. It seems that while the ashes of the destroyed island were flying through the air, the bottom of the sea was being vomited across the land.

If I live to be a great-great-grandmother, the oldest crone that has ever lived, I hope to never see a battle of the gods again.

But even though we can smell bonfires, and a stink of rotting sea creatures, there's no stench of dead animals or bodies like the miasma that hung over Tarmara. Maybe not so many died—or they have been buried or burned already. Maybe that's why the people of Gournia, although they're frightened, haven't rioted like the inhabitants of Tarmara.

One thing is for sure: there's a lot of work to do. And the time spent trapped in our goddess-shaken house, as well as the months on the farm, taught me that I'm strong. Even if I don't have great skills, I can lift and carry.

We start trying to help. I join a group of women hauling debris out of the ruins of a house, and they shout at me as if I'm going to steal these scraps of walls. A group of fishers collecting blocks of the floating pumice rocks are so shocked and confused when we try to help that their leader finally shoos us away. We try out our new story, but they don't seem to understand it and if they do, they don't believe it. The fishers' accent is much stronger than the craft-folk's, and we don't understand them much either.

After a while we give up, and they ignore us. They don't want us there but they don't chase us away, and they don't even mind Chance—we're nothing to them. Maybe they think Nunu and I have lost our spirits too, because Mama is not the only broken person on the beach. Many people are weeping quietly as they work; a young woman is standing waist-deep in the sea, screaming; an older man with a great scar across his forehead keeps going through the stack of salvage and laying it out across the beach. People mutter as they stack it up again and carry it up to safety, but no one shouts at him, or at the screaming woman in the sea—or at Mama chanting an endless "no, no, no."

But nothings don't get food and shelter; somehow we need to find our own. We need to survive before we can worry about belonging.

"We'll shelter for siesta, then go back to the town," I say. "We gave up too quickly—there must be something we can do there."

Towns are safer. Towns are what we know.

And the town holds Andras, the only person who's been kind to us.

"I could be a potter's apprentice, like his cousin," I say. The idea has been growing inside me, like a seed sprouting in a dark cupboard, and it feels like the first happy thought since the gods fought.

Nunu sniffs. I know that sniff. It means, *you don't know anything!*

"I have to do something, Nunu!"

But Nunu bursts into tears. "This is all wrong!" she sobs. "Your mama's spirit still wandering, you trying to work like a slave . . . and people saying the goddess has swallowed our home!"

It was better when I thought the sniff meant that I was wrong, and not the world.

"They're lying!" I insist. "You heard the sailors in Tarmara—the island that died didn't even have a town! It can't be ours. But for now . . . you know I always loved visiting your family's workshop. We'll be safe if I become an apprentice."

Nunu sniffs again and wipes her nose on her arm. "You could have made a much better jug than this," she says, and almost smiles.

For a moment it all seems easy. We'll find Andras and ask him to send us to the potter. We will sleep and eat with the other apprentices; I'll learn to make pots, beautiful pots, and when Dada returns I'll have a whole new supply of trade goods that I've made myself.

But the guard at the gate is the grumpy captain from the night before.

"The chief said we can enter the town," I tell him.

"Do you have a house to stay in?"

He knows we don't. I shake my head.

"Then you're within the walls only during the day. No beggars in the square overnight."

"We're not beggars!" I snap, at the same moment that Nunu says, "Goddess mercy, man, at least let us in to fill our waterjug. It's nowhere near nightfall."

Dogbreath smirks with satisfaction at making us beg. "You go, old one. These two and the dog stay outside to make sure you come back."

Hope disappears as fast as a frightened hare. Or maybe I'm the disappearing hare. I'm certainly frightened enough.

There's no point in asking if we can see Andras. He can't help us now. No one can.

We wait for Nunu to return with the precious jug of water, then go back to the ruin where we spent last night.

It's on a small point, with shrubby trees and prickly plants growing up through the floors that the ancients walked. A white cliff slopes steeply to the water, just on the edge of the fishers' beach. The fishers don't like us, but I don't think they'll harm us. That's the good part about being a nothing. On the other side of the bay, on the next point, is the stink of the purple village—the purple works, Andras called it.

But tonight the breeze is blowing from the west, blowing the smell away from us.

Inside, by a gap under a rock, is a snakeskin. This has been a good and maybe holy place: the house snake, the spirit of this home, is still here.

So I sing to the gods, pour a libation of fresh water from our ugly jug, and scatter a pinch of our dried chickpeas at the door. "Goddess of this point," I beg, "allow us to make a home here and honor the spirits of this place."

A feather drifts down. I look up to see three eagles circling.

Even Mama stands still, hand on heart in reverence until they disappear. The gods have given us permission to stay.

The fishers wouldn't let us help them, but they'd showed us what we had to do.

We eat our last barley cakes, Mama and I have a drink of water—"I drank at the well," says Nunu—then we cross to the cliff.

Just below is a ledge scattered with red, black, and gray pumice, the strange floating stones that the fishers are collecting to mend their houses. That's what we're going to do too.

Nunu agrees but Chance doesn't. He barks frantically, darting at me and nipping my hands when I scramble over the edge of the cliff. I'd tie him up if we hadn't lost his cord.

Ignoring him, I choose the first rock—a red one, as big as I can hold. Nunu starts to follow me, but this time I think Chance is right:

"I'll pass them up to you!"

Nunu lies down, and when she finally inches right to the edge of the cliff, grumbling all the way, manages to take the rock from me. Then Mama, as if her wandering spirit has been touched by the gods' eagles, takes the rock from Nunu and carries it to the ruin.

The rocks are light but the work is hard, and I don't want to be on the cliff when the sun disappears. I clamber back up: "Yes, yes!" says Mama, patting my face and showing me her pile of rocks. Chance throws himself at me, licking my face and hands with relief that I'm alive.

Nunu takes a bit longer to get to her feet and walk, stiff-legged and rubbing her back, over to the pile. I haul Chance back before he can jump at her and knock her down again.

The pile is as high as my waist, and as round as it's high. If Mama had put it next to a wall it could have been useful where it was. But she didn't, so we start stacking them to make two more walls to enclose the corner. My hands are scratched and sore before we start, bleeding when we stop — and we've only finished the pile, not the walls. It's easy enough to put them on the bottom, but it gets harder and harder to balance them with each layer. Still, even if each wall doesn't go much past my knees, we've got four of them, with a narrow space for a door.

Mama has given up helping. She sits in the corner watching us and smoothing the ground around her. Last night we were too tired and worried even to do that, so maybe she knows what she's doing; it's hard to tell. She shoves twigs and stones against the wall, pats the dirt smooth with her hands. One stone seems to please her. It's shaped like an ibis egg cut in half, the smooth, rounded side fitting neatly into the palm of her hand.

Ibis egg! I'm drooling at the thought.

"Good girl," says Nunu, holding out her hand. "Give it to me."

Mama makes a face but obeys.

"It's a tool from the Old Ones," says Nunu, showing me the chipped edge. "The goddess is thanking us for that dagger — she's given your mama a knife."

"It's a strange knife," I say doubtfully. I'm still angry about the palace taking our beautiful bronze dagger and giving us a handful of barley cakes in return.

"Or an ax," says Nunu. "I don't know what the Old Ones called it, but it'll cut branches to make a roof for this hut."

I take the rock out to the bushes to try it in the last evening light. I hammer and saw, but what works best is to chew away at the branch with the tool's serrated edge till it's weak enough to break. Nunu helps me drag the branches back. We can make a roof with them later, when our walls are higher, but for tonight we shove them into the ground at the door and around the walls, a dark filigree as the red light of the setting sun glows through them. Then darkness comes and we huddle together again, one cloak on the bottom and the other on top, and sleep, waking to twitch at noises then sleep again, on and off till sunrise. Chance mightn't be old enough to defeat bandits, but his warmth is comforting beside me.

Dreams of a house
 built of Mama's bones
 glued with tears—
 though I see my Mama-child sleeping
 curled safe on the floor
 while Nunu weeps and guards
 so I must build around them—
 my bone-bricks tumble
 and I grab and replace them
 with bleeding hands.
Waking sobbing
 because it seems the floating stones—
 red, black, and gray like the cliffs of our home—
 are bones of the great mother,
 and this dream is telling me
 what I don't want to know.

But in the hard-working days,
 it's easy to shove
 the dream from my mind.
 I walk to town each morning
 like a peasant girl, to fill our ugly jug,
 because I am the strongest
 and it no longer matters
 who's mistress or slave –
 and because I would burst
 if I never saw anyone except Nunu and Mama.
The other girls at the well
 are too busy chatting to bother with me—
 though they look me up and down—
 but Andras smiles,
 asks where we're living
 and if we've found work—
 we all know that work means food.
"The fishers are bringing in fish again," he says—
 though why would they feed us
 when they have barely enough
 for themselves?
But, as I step carefully home—
 the walk is too far
 to spill precious water—
 I wonder if Andras is saying
 that we could fish too.
I wish I'd spied
 on the boys in their Learning—
 my own Dada teaching them to fish
 and why couldn't he have taken me!

Just for fun, just in case,
because you never know
when you might lose everything
you've ever known.
And though I've watched the little boats
in our harbor,
it was never important to see
how they flicked their lines or nets,
or reeled in their catch.
Mama's muttering crossly,
    thinking I don't understand
    how hungry she is,
    as she follows me to the fishers' beach
    so I can watch and learn.
A few brave fishers are out on their boats
    but many have lost them—
    they wade to their waists
    in the sea that's taken their homes and living,
    bending and scooping,
    a patient dance with glistening nets;
    my heart dances too
    when I see fish leaping silver inside—
    I know the fish are dying
    but the fishers will live
    and if I can learn, so will we.
On the littered shore,
    others scavenge sad remains—
    a cry of joy at a paddle undamaged
    under the rubble of houses—
    and under that, a net.

The woman lifts it,
examines;
hugs it to her like a long-lost child—
a fishing net is not quick to weave
and the maker knows it for her own.
   Through my hopeless thought
      of how could we ever find or make one
      flashes an image, silver as leaping fish,
      of Mama bending and swooping
      in the swallow dance with her fishnet shawl.

I whisper my plan to Nunu. "But Mama will cry," I say.
   "Better than dying," says Nunu, taking the shawl from my mother's shoulders. "Time to wash it," she says, in her no-arguing voice, and Mama nods obediently.
   But sometimes Mama forgets that we don't have slaves and servants to do the work for us. She looks around the naked fishers on the beach, as if asking where the washing girls are.
   "I'll take it to them," I say quickly.
   Mama raises a disapproving eyebrow, just the way she used to—and I can't help it, I'm laughing. We haven't eaten since the day before yesterday, we're sleeping in a ruin with no roof—our whole world is broken and lost—but my mother is worrying about why the washing girls haven't appeared. For that tiny moment, I'm out of time, the way Pellie and I used to be when we laughed until our knees were weak and our eyes were leaking. I remember the feeling of clinging to each other, our heads bumping with the

force of our giggles, and the more our mothers raised their eyebrows, the harder we laughed. For an even tinier moment, I can feel Pellie here with me now.

Maybe she's laughing at home, and thinking of me. When we meet again we'll say, "Do you remember a day in spring when you started laughing for no reason, the way we did when we were children?" And that will make us laugh and cling to each other again, even though we'll be women by then.

But if I'm going to live long enough to be a woman, right now I need to play with the boys' Learning, and catch us a fish.

I head around the point with the fishnet shawl, away from Mama's disapproving eyebrow and the fishers' eyes. Chance stares in shock for a full two heartbeats, his head tilted on one side because he's forgotten ever hearing me laugh, and then bounds after me. I'm glad.

I untie my skirt, pull my nightshift over my head, and step naked into the sea. The cold water makes me gasp. I wade out deeper, till the water's as high as my chest, while Chance races up and down the beach, barking for me to come back. After a while he gives up and starts sniffing for anything to eat. He's not fussy about how long things have been dead.

The fishers' bending and scooping dance isn't as easy as it looks. No matter how I hold the net, it keeps floating to the surface; I bend deeper and splash stinging water into my eyes. I step back—my foot slides on something, the sand gives way, and I'm falling backwards, sitting on the seabed with my head under water, scrambling up coughing, spluttering, spitting out the taste of sea ...

I can't give up.

I find a firmer footing. It feels safer with the sea lapping no higher than my waist, and I can pull the net lower through the water without getting my face wet. Though sometimes I splash myself to cool off—the water doesn't feel so cold now I've fallen in, and the sun is warm behind the haze. My body settles into the rhythm of bending to pull the net through the water, scooping it up, starting again ...

And now I'm pulling it up and there's a little silver fish inside, and I'm so surprised I almost let go of the net. But I don't. I pull it in tight, and the little fish is mine.

"Mama!" I shout—I don't care about the disapproving eyebrow anymore. "I've caught a fish!"

I'm wading to shore as Mama and Nunu come around the point, and Mama starts *no, no, no*-ing at the sight of her daughter coming out of the water as naked as a fisher, until she sees what I'm carrying. "Fish!" she shrieks, her first word finally making sense. "Fish, fish, fish!"

I want to hand it to her, this amazing gift, but the tiny fish slips from the net and flops on the sand until Nunu hits it with a rock.

"Fish!" Mama exclaims again—and grabs it and eats it. It's very little. Two bites and it's gone—Mama is spitting out sand and saying, "fish, fish?" in a way that obviously means, *more, more!*

I go back out, and before the sun is high I've caught enough for us all to eat. We've each eaten two before I remember to thank the fish for giving their lives, so I sing a long prayer, praising the goddess for how wonderful a small raw fish can taste, wet and salty as the sea itself.

But after the first two, I think longingly of the smoky crispness of the fish Cook Maid used to serve us at home.

If only the fish could have cooked in the sun as easily as I did. My back and shoulders are red as a painted boy's, and sting where my shift touches them. I'm so thirsty I drained the last of our jug, and feel like crying to think I'll have to walk all the way back to the well for more.

But that's what I do, even though everyone else in the world is having their siesta, because I'm too thirsty to rest. I return even hotter, more tired, and impatient to have a home. Nunu and I get more rocks and build our walls higher: they're growing well till one rock rolls out from the bottom and that whole wall crashes down.

Mama watches thoughtfully, eating a lizard.

I'll have to fish again tomorrow.

My skin burns like fire. Blisters pop up on my sore snub nose and across my shoulders. I want to spend the day lying in a soft bed in a cool dark room, with a maid bringing me grapes, cheese, and sweet wet ale . . .

I'm down at the sea in time to greet the dawn; the water is cool but Nunu wraps me in a cloak when I get out with my meager morning catch. It doesn't take long to eat.

And we need water again. I've never understood how constant the need for water is. Nunu helps me drop my nightshift over my head so it doesn't catch on my blistered shoulders and wraps my skirt around me. It goes around further than it used to. I think about draping my cloak over my head to protect my sunburned face but the woollen fabric is too heavy — and I'd look even less like a servant who could be offered work.

Which doesn't matter anyway, because Dogbreath is at the gate. "Get your water and get out. You won't get work or rations till you're in the homeless camp!"

The camp is even bigger, noisier, and smellier than before. It's like the animal sheds at the farm when everyone started getting sick. If we went there, Mama would wail, we'd be driven out, ostracized or worse . . . I still don't know if that was a joke about Chance being dinner.

I drink at the well, refill my jug, and leave.

But the fish I can catch with my shawl net are barely enough to keep us alive. The fishers are our only hope.

Down at the shore, everyone who's not fishing or building is picking sea greens. The murdering wave ripped them from their rocks, scattering them high on the shore to rot, but they're already growing again. And though they're precious as gold, the only greens anywhere not smothered by ash, the fishers say nothing when we begin gathering too.

They trust us! I think. I'm surprised at how good that feels.

"No!" shouts a tall, strong-looking woman, charging at Mama and grabbing something out of her hand.

Nunu and I rush at them. Rage roars through me, fiercer and stronger because of that fleeting thought of trust. "Don't you dare touch my Mama!"

Mama is screeching and trying to snatch her treasure back.

"Bad," the woman tells her. "Make you sick. Make you die." She shows us a rotting oyster on an open shell, before flinging it as far away as she can.

My anger dissolves into tears. "Thank you," I say, with my hand on my heart, and Nunu does the same.

The woman nods. Then she takes us around the beach, pointing out the sea greens and shell creatures that are good to eat, and the ones that aren't. I pay attention as if this was Kora with the next step of my Learning.

"Priest-folk know nothing," the fisherwoman says suddenly.

Nunu laughs and I blush.

"But you're not priest-folk now—you can learn."

I'm glad that Mama hasn't understood. I don't know if I understand either: I'm still Leira, and my clan is part of who I am, or who I used to be . . . It's a good thing the fisherwoman isn't waiting for an answer.

"They say you're living in the home of the Old Ones?"

I nod.

"And that you have no fire?"

I nod again.

She beckons us to follow her up to a half-built shelter of salvage and pumice, like ours. The fire beside it has been banked for the day, a big log smouldering gently under a layer of sand, but she takes a stick and pokes it in till it's glowing.

We have fire.

The moon has cycled from full to full again since the war of the gods, but my bleeding hasn't cycled with it. It's come with the new moon, every time since it started. Mama said that was a sign of power.

I've gone from maiden to crone, old as Nunu, without ever being a woman in between.

I don't want to tell Nunu, but Nunu always knows. And I don't want to cry, but I do. "What's happened? Am I old?"

"Not old," says Nunu grimly. "Just hungry. Your body needs food for its magic."

My first bleeding, in the House of the Lady,
    learning a woman's blood is sacred,
    her body a mystery

known only to the goddess—
who transforms that blood into life.
To be a maiden, an almost-woman,
    not strong enough to bleed,
    dishonors the goddess—
    and I never want to see
    our great mother angry again.
The fish I catch with Mama's shawl
    are barely enough to keep us alive;
    the sea greens no more than a taste
    and no green grows yet on the ashy hills.
At the town,
    even the kind guards answer the same:
    "No one new enters the palace;
    no servants needed—
    especially one from the island
    we dare not name."
I can see Andras in the workshop—
    it's not far from the well
    if you take the wrong path.
    His head bent over his work,
    hair long enough to plait
    pulled back from his face
    as he smooths a stone
    for his mother to carve.
    "Wait!" he calls—
    and what else do I have to do?
    I watch and wait
    and wish.
"Are you buying?" calls the carver—
    a small woman, with such tiny hands

I wonder that she can hold her tools
with the strength to cut stone.
"Not today," I say, before I hear her laughter,
    because for a moment
    I was back in Tarmara
    planning the trade goods I'd buy and sell
    not the hungry beggar she sees.
Andras shows her the stone;
    she studies it with fingers and eyes,
    nods in approval.
    "You can fetch more water from the well
    but I don't want to wait
    because someone walks with you."
He flushes, and escapes.
    "She's kinder than most," he says,
    carrying his pitcher—not as ugly as ours—
    and just for a moment I hope:
    "Would she take me as apprentice?"
"We've never had anyone
    outside the family,
    and she doesn't know how
    we'll trade what we have
    if the world stays hungry as now."
Home with my jug and aching heart
    I ask the tall fisherwoman
    if I can learn to fish with them,
    but she laughs and says,
    "You mayn't be priest-folk now
    but you're no fisher neither."
A changing breeze
    wafts a stink of purple up my nose—

choking, putrid stench of rot—
but even purple slaves
have food.

In night dreams I am small,
　　a lowly snail
　　that Mama wants to eat,
　　grabbing me from my path—
　　her round mouth opens,
　　teeth sharp as a wolf's—
　　but Nunu shouts, "No!"
　　and pulls me away from Mama's grasp,
　　throwing the me-snail as far
　　as her arm is strong
　　because I am stinking rotten
　　and no one who eats me
　　will survive.
The thrown snail flies free,
　　losing its shell to become a swallow
　　while the empty shell falls
　　to grow like barley,
　　rich and golden
　　in the purple earth.

13

Andras is at the gate, which makes me feel more hopeful and more embarrassed at the same time. I'm glad that I'm clean and my skirt is tied neatly over my used-to-be white shift; I'm embarrassed because I'm planning a lie.

"I want to be listed with the homeless, to be assigned work," I tell him.

His face lights up; I can tell he has good news before he says it. "I've heard the palace needs more servants, now that everything's calmer and they know what needs doing."

"I could be a servant!"

"Like you used to be, in that town near Tarmara?" A shared secret as well as a warning—not that I'm likely to forget. We've never mentioned our homeland again, and with my sunburned face, rough hands and torn shift, I could easily be a servant. My precious skirt is the only thing that could give me away, and even that is dirty.

"You'll have to see the labor guard," Andras adds.

"Aren't you the guard dog today?"

"Just for barking, not deciding." He grins.

The labor guard is Dogbreath, the bad tempered captain from the first night. "I told you before: you can't register for work or rations if you're not in the homeless camp," he says flatly. "How can we know where the workers are, if they're not all together?"

Even with my plan, the thought of the camp makes me shiver.

"I can see that doesn't suit you," he says slowly. "But I think there's a way I can help."

He's not as nasty as he looks, I think. I am giddy with relief.

My plan is simple: we'll go to the camp, but after dark on the first night, we'll escape to our home on the cliff top. Mama and Nunu can stay there, while I appear at the camp first thing every morning. As a maid in the palace I can earn enough rations for them both. They never need to go back to the camp.

"Andras!" Dogbreath barks suddenly. "Take your turn up at the watch-hill. I can cover the gate without you."

My friend—*can I call a boy a friend?*—looks surprised, but salutes us and leaves.

"I don't know where you got it, since you're not priest-women," says the guard, once Andras is out of sight, "but I've seen your mother wearing a gold chain."

The words chill like a blast of cold north wind.

"If I had that necklace, I could arrange for you to be

on the ration list without being in the camp—and make sure that you serve in a way that's fitting for you."

His smile is worse than his usual grumpy face.

No, no, no! That's Mama's birthing necklace; Dada gave it to her when she had Glaucus! I can't take that from her!

How will we survive if I don't?

Nunu finds a clam shell with a hole in the top, plaits reeds into a cord, and gives Mama her new necklace. Mama loves it. She keeps showing me how pretty it is. She barely notices when I take the gold one from her neck.

"Don't cry!" Nunu snaps at me, wiping her face with the back of her hand. "Your mama understands more than you think."

I go back to the gates. Andras is still nowhere in sight. Dogbreath holds out his hand.

"For this, I want rations for all three of us when I work."

He grumbles, but can't take his eyes off the gold chain. "Rations for three," he agrees, and I drop the necklace into his hand. He tucks it into a pouch on his belt.

I will not cry in front of him.

He's grinning again. The north-wind feeling returns.

"I said I'd send you where it's fitting, and I'll keep my promises. It's not right for you to be in the palace, after what the chief and Lady decreed. Did you think I'd forgotten where you said you'd come from? The place for you is the purple works, where no one knows or cares who you were before. I'll put the three of you on their ration list for tomorrow—be there at sunrise."

I hate him, I hate him, I hate him!

I didn't know I could feel so much rage against one person. It feels as if I've swallowed the great mother's fire and am about to spew it all over him.

But I can't. I have to swallow the fire down again, no matter how sick it makes me, because that's the only way we'll survive.

14

Chance's howling fades behind me; I hope Nunu's still holding tight to his collar, almost as much as I wish I had him by my side. I stumble as the first light begins to glint through the gray, and tears leak from my eyes. Or maybe it's just the eye-watering stench, worse with every step. I sing the dawn as I walk, even though I don't want the sun to rise, don't want to get where I'm going.

The purple works are further away than I thought, and bigger. There are shelters for slaves, houses for dyers and well-built warehouses, far enough from the shore that they weren't damaged in the flood. Or maybe the giant wave didn't enter this sheltered cove inside the wider harbor—whatever the reason, this place survived better than anywhere else I've seen since that terrible night. Now it's busy as a harbor on a sailing day. Dripping naked divers carry baskets up from the sea, squatting slaves in loincloths hammer shells with rocks, tripod cauldrons hiss over fires, clouds of stinging wasps and buzzing flies hover over pots of purple slime, overseers shout and people cry and curse at hammered fingers or stung noses.

"The palace has sent me to work here."

A small, pig-nosed man at the entrance studies me as if he can't understand my words.

I try to look calm and confident. Try not to flap my hands at the flies, and most of all, try not to choke. *Like the morning of the saffron picking—trying to sing the great mother's praises and ignore her burping.*

It's the only thing that is like that morning. This smell is worse than the earthmother's belch; it's more disgusting than anything from this world should be. It fills the air like smoke, smothers like ash, attacks like an animal, burrowing into my skin. I will never be clean again.

"I've been sent to work here," I repeat, more slowly and loudly in case he's deaf. Being deaf would be a blessing, with the overwhelming din. Though not being able to smell would be better. "I can weave," I add hopefully.

Pignose laughs. "You think weavers work out here? If the palace wanted you to weave, you'd be in town. That's where the wool gets spun and woven—they don't send the fabric out till it's ready to be dyed."

"I'll do other work," I say, ignoring the panicked voice in my head: *What other work?*

"Maybe you've apprenticed as a dyer?" He sneers, because of course he knows I haven't. "It's slaves as work here. So if you've run away from a mistress in town, go back and face your beating—there's nothing fit for you here."

"I have no mistress," I say, my face glowing like a liar's though I'm telling the truth. "My home is gone, and my people, except for my mama and grandmother." I suppose Nunu's a slave, but grandmother actually seems truer now as well as safer. "My mama is like a child since the earth shook; I must care for all of them. That's why I went to the labor captain yesterday. He assigned me here and put us down for rations for the three of us, for my work."

Pignose's face twists as if he's adding something up, and settles into smugness as he decides. "Palace don't want you, nor town nor fishers. You're not used to working and you've got no skills—you're not worth one slave's rations, let alone three. But if that's what the palace says, I'll find work for you, with shelter and rations for the others."

Shelter in the slave quarters! Mama cried at the thought of the homeless camp, but this would kill her.

"We don't need shelter."

"Don't think the folks at camp will let you back in when you're working here!"

"We'll stay where we are." There's no reason to tell him we're not at the camp. I don't want him to know any more about me than he has to.

He shrugs. "All the same to me where you sleep. But if you're not here for headcount every sunrise, all three of you will be thrown out to starve."

"I'll be here."

"I'll be here!" he mimics, in a squeaky voice that sounds nothing like me.

Am I supposed to laugh? Salute? I do nothing.

"You start with them, off to the hills to get bait for the traps." He points to two small boys and a girl, none of them more than seven summers old.

I can surely manage anything they can.

"Remember: the rottener the better, that's what the beasties like. You fill these baskets or there'll be no rations—but even folk as used to be priests must know how to follow the vultures."

He stares to see how I react; he wants to humiliate me as much as he can. He wants to tell me I'm a slave.

I'm not! I'm not a slave, because I can leave. There's nothing forcing me to come back tomorrow.

Except starvation.

But I'm still me, Leira! I'm not a slave and I never will be!

I pick up the filthy baskets and follow the naked children into the hills. Out of sight of Pignose and the works, I untie my beautiful flounced skirt, fold and hide it under a rock. *A rock by the root of the only olive tree on this hill, where I can see the sea to the north and the town to the south . . .* I paint it into my mind, to make sure I can find it again tonight.

Without my skirt to cover it, the loose sides of my nightshift flap in the breeze. It's already well shredded from catching on thorns and prickles all the way across the mountains—a few more rips and there'll be nothing left from the waist down.

I tuck the back between my knees, knotting it with the front into loose pants. I'm covered from neck to thighs, in a place where no one else is wearing more than a loincloth—but even out of sight of anyone except these three naked children, I feel bare and ridiculous. And humiliated. Completely, absolutely, overwhelmingly humiliated.

The children watch me warily.

"My skirt," I tell them. "Nobody touch."

They look so frightened I relent. "What are you called?"

Their thin little faces fill with terror and confusion.

How can they not know their own names?

"I'm Leira," I say, which seems to confuse them even more. I don't try again. If they don't know about names I'm guessing they don't know what a skirt is. I'll just hope it'll be safe till tonight. *Why did I wear it? Why was I so stupid to think I'd be allowed to weave if I looked decent?*

We trudge on, heading east into the sun until the purple stink fades enough that we can breathe. Maybe this isn't a bad job after all.

Suddenly the taller boy, whose right foot twists in at a funny angle, grunts and points. Vultures are circling, flapping down to something on the ground. The children are almost running toward it. Running *toward* a vulture! Are they crazy?

"Stop!" I shout. Pignose said follow the vultures— not fight with them!

I've never been so close to one. Their heads are white but their bodies glow red in the dim sun, as if

225

their chests are smeared with blood. Stories tell of them snatching babies from parents to feed to their own young, and I wonder if it's only babies—their black wings spread wider than Dada's arms.

But the children don't care that they're barely as tall as the birds. They pick up branches and whirl them over their heads, racing shrieking toward whatever is lying on the ground. The birds flap away, one of them carrying a long bloody bone.

Whatever it used to be—a goat or an ibex, I hope— has been dead for longer than I can guess. Up close, it stinks nearly as disgusting as the purple works. The children dash in to cram lumps of putrid flesh into their baskets. Turning, they stare and wait for me to do the same.

That's what we're here for: collect rotten meat to bait the traps. Just do it.

I'm not touching it.

I find a rock to scrape it up with, lean over the remains—and vomit.

The children laugh so hard I'm surprised they don't throw up too.

Now the smell of my own vomit is added to the stench of rot. The sight of it makes me gag, but I try again, poking flesh onto my rock with a stick. The children think this is even funnier than vomiting onto it, but eventually I manage to fill my baskets—without ever touching the rottenness or being sick again.

The baskets are heavy; we walk back slowly, the smell growing again as we draw closer. I was wrong about the dead smell in the hills being as bad as this. Nothing stinks like this. I start toward the gates but the children shake their heads violently, grunting in fear.

Fear is what it means to be a slave. I don't know what the punishment would be for walking into the works, like I thought I was supposed to, instead of following the children down to the beach. I don't have to know — I've already caught their fear.

Out in the deeper waters of the cove, divers jump off small fishers' boats. Just when I'm sure they must have drowned, they burst up again, clinging to the side with one hand and passing the end of a rope to the fisher on board. The diver catches his breath as the fisher hauls, shoves the dripping basket-trap onto the boat, and dives again.

Sometimes the trap slips off the boat and sinks like a stone — a real stone, not a floating bone of a dead island — trailing its rope behind it. One young fisher boy catches the rope when that happens and is pulled overboard with it. The older men know to wait for the diver to bring it up again, though one overbalances as he helps haul the trap on board, and the little boat flips upside-down, throwing out its cargo of full traps as well as the men. Two other divers swim over to help; the boat is shoved right way up, and the fisher scrambles back on board, splashing water out with his hands. The divers disappear into the sea to find the ropes and start hauling the traps up again.

As the boats return to shore, the divers haul their traps onto the beach and start sorting the contents.

Eels and a few small fish are kept aside to be cooked and eaten, and finally the murex shellfish—the reason for all this activity as well as the stink—are thrown into baskets to be taken up to the works where they can be turned into precious purple dye. I expect them to be purple, but their heavy whorled shells are mud colored, and the meat inside is the brown of most shell creatures.

A piercing scream. A diver clearing a trap is writhing on the shore.

"Scorpion fish!" The shout is echoed around the beach as the other divers race to him.

I point my fingers against evil. I remember Dada in the sea god's beautiful shrine room, talking to Mama when they didn't know I was listening, still a child too young to know that grown-ups could cry. "These evil fish look like stones," he'd said. "One of my young sailors stepped on one when he jumped off the ship to haul her in. The pain was fast but the death was slow, and such agony he begged me to kill him. To my shame, I couldn't."

Mama murmured something I couldn't hear, but Dada was louder.

"I swore to the gods that if it happened again, I'd have the courage and face their consequences."

The divers are keening as if the bitten man is already dead, but one bends over him, ear to lips and they all pause to listen. One by one, they touch his forehead and then their own hearts, and the keening changes to a hymn I've never heard.

God of the cove, father of the deep,
guardian of creatures
who swim and crawl
giving their lives
to bring life and death,
we praise your bounty
and offer one of our own,
freed now from slave life.
God of the cove, take him,
free him from pain.
God of the cove, keep him,
in your home in the deep.
God of the cove, spare us
that we can worship you more.

The bitten diver's arm is red and swollen to the shoulder; his screams crescendo and subside. Still singing, four men lift his writhing body gently onto a boat and push it out to sea. Two climb on with him, one to hold him steady and the other to paddle. The other divers and fishers — everyone on the beach except the three children and me, and the pig-nosed overseer striding down from the works — take their boats and paddle out in a procession behind them.

Like a funeral procession — except he's not dead.

We can still hear the singing when they reach the rougher water where the cove meets the wider harbor. The men's forms are blurred as they slide the diver into the sea, but his thrashing and struggles are clear. They sing as they return too, but not so loudly. Most are weeping.

"What are you waiting for?" snaps Pignose.

Face of a pig, soul of a vulture.

The sun is past its peak as we hand over our baskets; the divers drop stinking bits of rotten ibex into the empty traps, and head back out on their little boats to lay the traps again. We pick up their baskets of fresh murex, carry them up to the works and dump them into big pots with a pitcher of sea water.

A gong sounds.

"Food!" says the little girl.

It's the only clear word I've heard any of the children say.

The food is a sort of fish and sea-greens stew of every edible thing caught in the traps, and the remains of the big murex when their dye gland has been pulled out. The overwhelming stink has invaded my mouth and tongue as well as my nose, so I have no idea what this tastes like, but it is hot and filling.

The children slip away. I'm just wondering where we rest for the siesta, when the overseer bellows at me. "Over here, Not-a-Priestess!"

He thinks that's funny. I won't show him I care.

He points me to a group of people sitting on a flat stone around a pot of murex. "Show her what to do," he orders.

A one-eyed man dumps the shellfish out of the pot, and hands me a rock.

"Smash the little ones and throw them back into the pot," says a girl, not much older than me. In fact, no one is much older than me. I don't think there's a person in the works over twenty summers, not even Pignose.

I pound and pound before I figure out that only the smallest shells can be smashed. If they're even as long as my thumb the only way to get the dye is by hammering a bronze pin through the side and wiggling the mucky gray gland out through the hole—without pricking yourself with the pin. The hammerers' fingers are quick and skilled, but they are also bruised and bloody, and most have missing fingernails.

I'm too lowly to be trusted with a pin. My fingers are scratched and sore, but by the end of the day, when the pot is full of thick purple sludge, I still have my fingernails.

The fish stew is served again at sunset. I gulp mine down, and refill the bowl for Mama and Nunu. The cook lets me light a branch at the fire, and with that in one hand and the stew in the other, I head the long way back across the hills. I am so tired I can hardly walk.

Nunu and Mama burst into tears when they see me. "Oh, my child!" says Nunu, as if she's speaking for them both.

She's definitely speaking for them both when she adds, "Your mother needs you to leave your shift outside for the night. We'll hang it over the thorn bush to air—I don't think even a wolf will take it!"

She wraps me in my cloak as I strip off, and takes my stinky shift outside. I stink too, but I'm asleep before they finish eating their stew.

And I leave again in the morning before Mama
wakes.

*

I don't know how I've offended the gods
    to make them hate me like this
    but I must have done something—
    or not done something I should—
    because the life I'm living
    is nearer death than life.
My spirit wanders,
    not caring if it's lost as Mama's
    and never finds my body—
    this body that lives in muck
    hammering with rocks and bruised fingers,
    this body that stumbles in sleep
    trudging home to its mama
    who cries at its stink.
But Nunu has earned the fishers' trust,
    cares for babies while mothers work,
    helps tend the injured and ill,
    with Mama by her side
    or wandering, watched by all.
The fishers feed them as their own—
    they don't need the stew I carry,
    earned with such pain.
Chance finds his own feed,
    guards Mama and Nunu at night
    and no longer howls when I leave.

Do they even miss me
   the nights it seems easier
   to sleep on the slave floor,
   knowing I will never be free?
Some days I hear Pellie,
   more real than grunting children
   or frightened slaves;
   more real than me.
   She scolds and teases
   that her friend is not destined
   for a purple life—
   she doesn't say whether
   the purple is priesthood or slavery—
   and how can she know?
She hasn't choked on this stink,
   hasn't felt the blow
   of a stick on her back
   for falling asleep as she works,
   hasn't pounded her fingers
   with a hammer of rock,
   hasn't tripped and fallen on a path at night
   and lain there till dawn
   because her legs won't move.
And if Pellie knows
   how long I've been here,
   she doesn't tell me,
   though another full moon comes;
   maybe another—
   and still I don't bleed.
   I know now
   I'll never be a true woman.

But this morning her voice is clear
   through the crash of hammers:
   "The goddess calls; Nunu needs you.
   You must see your mama."
"You're not an oracle!" I snap—
   One-Eye hears me
   but doesn't care if I'm crazy
   as long as I smash my shells.
When the night stew is eaten
   I cross the hills
   to do what my friend says.
The wailing reaches me far from our hut:
   Mama's high, Nunu's deeper,
   lu-lu-lu-ing the grief of broken hearts—
   I don't know how many times
   a heart can break.
"Traders came today," Nunu weeps.
   "The tall goldsmith from our town
   is travelling with them,
   searching for a place to work his craft.
   He said that when the great mother's belching
   had the stink of death
   and steam was hissing from her home,
   he and as many as could fit
   left on the other ships
   the dawn before the war of the gods.
"What the sailors said is true:
   it was our island torn apart,
   her heartland scattered
   and all souls on her
   swallowed in fire and ash."

"No!" I scream,
    and again like Mama,
    "No, no, no!
    The sailors said
    there was no town or harbor
    on the island that died!"
"The earthmother's fire
    spewed rock and ash
    from the depths of her belly—
    our town and its harbor
    are buried deep
    under a mountain."

15

Nunu's words come through a haze. I can't seem to hear them, and when I do hear, I can't understand. This is too huge, too impossible, to be true—and I am too black and empty inside to feel anything at all. Something in me is broken and will never be right.

Mama doesn't need to understand words. She wails in pure grief. Nunu is crushed and pale; her face twists as she repeats the goldsmith's words, as if she's reliving the horror of his memories herself. Her story is incoherent with sobs. Maybe his was too.

A sudden thought, like a flash of light through my darkness: The goldsmith said everyone who could fit was on that ship: *Pellie's nearby! That's why I've been hearing her in my head!*

"Where are the Lady and her family now?"

"The Lady said the ship must wait till the next dawn, for the rituals of sailing season. The captain was like your dada—he knew they couldn't wait."

"The Swallow Clan didn't board?" I hear my voice, a whisper in the distance. "None of them?"

Nunu shakes her head. "None, nor my family neither. Goldsmiths and jewelers is all; and the sailors and their families."

"But it doesn't mean they died! They'd have fled to the hills and farms again. They're safe on the other side of the mountain, Nunu, I know they are!"

"No one was safe." Her voice drops to a whisper, as if she's afraid of her own words. "The goldsmith's skin is scarred by the rain of embers, far out to sea though they were. Fire and rock poured onto the island and the sea around it. Boats burned on the waves. There are mountains now where once were fields; cliffs where once was shore. Nothing lives—the island is gone, child, as sure as if it's sunk under the sea."

My mind is blacker than the night around us—
   this time the truth won't be pushed away.
   I told Pellie she was no oracle
   but perhaps she is,
   her spirit voice in my head
   all of her that is left.
And still my mind screams
   because how can Pellie,
   all of her family,
   Ibi's wife and his baby,
   the farmers who cared for us—
   everyone we've ever known—

be gone as if
they never were?
I can't believe it
and I won't.

Mama and Nunu sob through the night,
but it seems that I slept
because Nunu is shaking me awake
and I run stumbling
through a morning gray as my soul
for the headcount at dawn.
I know now why slaves don't speak—
there are no words
for the loss of all hope,
for a life without joy
that is no life at all.
I move through the day
of gathering rot
and hammering shells
and if I could feel
I would be one of the creatures
crushed between rocks—
but I cannot even feel pain.
Though I'm wrong that slaves can't feel—
there is a ripple, almost of joy,
when the overseer with his cruel pig face
says that midsummer comes tomorrow
and the Lady has declared
that even the slaves—
no-good and lazy as we are, he adds—

will honor the great mother
and the sun still pale from the war of gods;
call them to strength on this longest day—
though the priest-folk,
processing in purple,
don't want the stink of the slaves who made it
so we will honor her here
with what song and praise
such lowly creatures can offer.
Pellie's voice says clear:
   "A day of song and praise
   will have no headcount,"
so I stumble home again at dusk.
I have no plan,
   but Pellie does.

It feels so good to wake next to Mama and know that I don't have to return to the purple works for a day, that I snuggle against her like a child. But Mama moans in her sleep and I don't need Pellie's voice to tell me to wash. I rescue my stinking shift from its thorn bush outside our door—Nunu was right, no human or animal has ever tried to steal it—and pull it on to go down to our secluded beach.

Mama and Nunu have been invited to honor the fishers' goddess with them, but Pellie has other plans for me.

The morning is warming already, though the water is still cold at first step. I pull off my shift and drop it into the shallows; wade out further.

"Undo your plait and get your head under the water!" orders Pellie.

If she wasn't a spirit I'd argue back. But she is, so I duck under and splutter up, splashing and scrubbing, over and over, letting my ponytail and forelock float free. The sea warms around me, holding and rocking, washing me clean; my body relaxes as if it doesn't know that nothing will ever melt the frozen blackness inside. Lights dance on the water as the sun struggles to rise from behind the hills to the east, far beyond the purple works. I sing the dawn, alone out here in the water, though from beyond the point I can hear the fishers singing their own song, Mama and Nunu with them.

What am I doing alone on this sacred day? Why aren't I with my family?

"You're doing what the great mother bids," says Pellie. "Your way is not with the fishers."

"Or the priest-folk or the craft-folk or the slaves," I snap back, but go on singing, even though I'm too numb to care whether the sun becomes strong or gives us this longest day of the year.

The day that I should have been starting the fourth and final season of becoming a woman, celebrating rites that I will never learn, for a land that no longer exists.

"You'll learn if you listen!" says Pellie.

I pull my shift out of the shallows and shake it. Something white flies free, and I catch it mid-air, my hand snatching before I have time to think, the way it did when Pellie and I danced with balls, throwing them back and forth to each other, four small balls in the air at once.

This one is just a pebble, smooth and white, perfectly round and no wider than a fingernail. It's not gold or a jewel, but I would wear it as a necklace if I could; use it as my seal-stone. Even my frozen heart knows that it comes from Pellie. I will keep it forever.

So I pull on my damp shift, finger-comb the curls that flow past my ears now, and tease out the tangles of the long hank before tying it into its bouncing ponytail again. No plait today; even hair needs to dance wild and free to celebrate the goddess in her strength. I retrieve my sacred skirt from the hut and wrap it around me, the flounces falling straight and the waist wrapped tight. My pebble is knotted securely into the tail of the sash; whether Pellie is oracle or friend, I need her with me.

I'm as ready as I can be, though I'm glad there's no mirror.

I still don't know what I'm ready for.

"You must climb to the goddess's mountain shrine," says Pellie.

"But the rituals were at dawn! And I'm not allowed."

"The people are returning now. You'll not be seen, but the goddess will hear you."

"I've already given everything we have. I've got nothing left!"

"There is always something left," Pellie says firmly, in her oracle voice.

The peak shrine is clear from here. There are taller mountains, but this one is a perfect, rounded cup of a hill. It will be two hours of walking before I get to the base.

I think Pellie's spirit will guide me, but she has disappeared; maybe she thinks I don't need her now. The town is deserted as I pass, and the trail to the mountain is wide. Sometimes it twists so that I can see the snake-line of people winding down toward me, too far away to tell how many or how fast they're walking.

Then I hear the music: the chanting of ecstatic song, from the Lady's clear soprano to the chief's deepest bass, threaded through with the piping of flutes and the clatter of rattles.

How far away? I ask Pellie.

No answer.

I keep going, peering around each bend before I step, and am at the foot of the mountain before I see the first priest-folk coming toward me. I can tell the Lady and the chief because there are guards in front and behind them, but even the guards are chanting. There's time to wrap my skirt more tightly around me, scramble through two thorn bushes and rest with my back to a tree.

I don't know if I'm allowed to be here, or if it matters if they see me. I just know that I need to do this, and do it alone.

The bushes around me are too thick to push through; I'll have to wait till the path is safe. I curl up in the dirt between the roots of the tree, and doze in the shade.

When I wake, the sun is close to its full height and the path is empty. I start to climb. The heat beneath the haze is kiln-hot and my throat is already dry—but I am tougher now than I've ever believed I could be. The trail is steep and the higher it goes, the more often it's nothing but rock to rock, a high step up where I'm guessing the Lady had the support of her guards so as not to bring ill omens with a stumble and fall.

I do it alone and I don't stumble—and though my parched throat won't sing loud, I hum the goddess's song under my breath.

Goddess of all
we sing your praise;
give us long days
for fruit and field.

Mother of all
we bring you gifts
give us long life
for flock and herd.

Since I don't have a gift, I sing the hymn over and over, the endless verses that list every fruit and grain, every green and growing thing that the sun's warmth will ripen and we will eat: olives and barley, pomegranates and lentils, because even those harvested in winter or spring need this midsummer heat to grow.

The rote words stop me thinking about my only true wish: take the world back to the way it was a year

ago, when all I had to worry about was when I would
start my bleeding and my Learning.

    Stepping off the path
        I shelter a moment in the arms of a rock
        so old it's been hollowed by gods
        like the huge trunk of a tree
        blasted open by lightning—
        and though it's a rock,
        it has the same god-feel
        as the wishing tree at home.
The shrine is clear from here:
        red pillars and doors
        into the side of the hill,
        the bull-horned altar
        with its splash of blood,
        the offerings around it—
        with vultures hovering—
        and the priestess-guardian
        in the shade of the wall.
Since the earth mother shook
        half a year ago, on the shortest day,
        I've done all that I could,
        lost more than I can believe,
        suffered more than I knew I could bear.
        Even now,
        clean and combed in my sacred skirt
        blood reddening my feet
        I've climbed the mountain alone
        offering my songs—
        and the goddess laughs.

Outcast that I am—
    neither priest nor slave—
    I cannot approach the shrine
    that the priestess guards.
I thought I was broken,
    dead inside and couldn't feel—
    but that numb deadness
    was deep as the sea—
    my rage is swelling like the murdering wave:
    red fury, weighted with darkness
    because it's Mama I hate
    for losing her spirit,
    Dada for leaving us;
    Glaucus for dying—
    and me for betraying my clan
    and becoming a slave.
But now, my body shaking
    like the earthmother's trembling,
    my fury erupts
    blinding and deafening
    like the gods at war;
    scorching my veins
    like the rain of fire
    that scarred the goldsmith;
    swallowing me like the burning rocks
    that killed my land,
    my clan, my friends, my home.
We are nothing—
    the chips the gods play with
    in their gambling games—

the only one to hate
is our goddess, mother of all.
She's betrayed us,
over and over,
not honoring the gifts
we sacrificed,
demanding her rites
as she destroys our world.
I shriek my fury—
if the priestess hears, I don't know or care—
I can't think or feel
anything but hate—
I scream until
the rage drains
and I feel the warm slither
of a snake across my toes—
messenger of the goddess,
from her world to ours.
"Follow," says Pellie.
"You must sink into darkness
before you can rise."
I don't know what she means
because Pellie
is no longer my sister-friend
but a spirit oracle.
Deep in my belly I know that she's gone
but am glad of her voice—
though I wish she'd still speak like my friend.
The snake disappears,
but a second trail leads from this rock;

I leave the path to the shrine
and follow the hill's great curve
to where the rocks gape open—
a door to the underworld,
the great mother's belly—
and I see the flick
of the snake as it enters.
I don't need Pellie to tell me to follow;
I've hated the great mother—
as well as my own
and now I must pay.
l follow the snake
into cool blackness,
walls wet with the mother's weeping,
and in the emptiness of caverns
touch pillars of tears,
growing as stone from ceiling and floor.
No light or sound, no heat nor time
nor scent of any living thing,
but I creep on and down
sliding on a foot-worn way;
heart thudding,
thick fear rising
entering the belly of the mother
with nothing to offer—
but my feet go on as Pellie ordered
slipping down in the blackness
past the tear-built rocks;
till I feel water rising to my knees
and am blinded by light—

a bolt from the sun at its peak
to the belly of the earth
lighting the pool I stand in
with the neglected rock altar
waiting for gifts.
I have no gold
or bronze or precious things—
nothing except myself—
like the fish-bitten diver
who took his agonies to the deep
and gave his life to the sea god.
The fishers will care
for Mama and Nunu;
there's no trade to be done
for a disappeared land—
and a purple slave
is no use to anyone.
And yet
there's a difference between
living a life that's no use
and leaving it forever.
I'm more afraid
than when the house fell
or the gods fought
or we fled the palace
because I can't see a priest or a knife
and I don't know how
the goddess will take me—
I only know
that I don't want to die.

"Great Mother," I plead,
    and for that moment of loving life,
    I forget my misery,
    the fatigue and fear of a purple slave,
    "let me live to serve you—
    if not as my clan, then however I can."
Standing in that pool, in the light
    with deepest darkness all around
    waiting for death, or a sign
    I go beyond fear;
    the world spins,
    my head so light it might float
    my gaze goes black
    and my body limp,
    falling and knowing that this is the end.
Waking spluttering, shivering
    in the cold pool of tears—
    adding mine to them—
    my bumped head so real I must be alive.
    I need to learn why.
Weak as a newborn,
    I drink and bathe
    in the great mother's tears;
    life flows through me, quick and strong,
    my ears so sharp I hear each drop
    trickling through caverns,
    my eyes so bright I see
    under the water,
    around the base of the neglected altar
    pretty pebbles and shells, left for the goddess

who doesn't need gold or jewels
but a perfect offering from the heart.
"I have nothing," I've said,
but that's not true.
In a knot at the end of my sash
is the sea-polished pebble,
Pellie's gift that speaks
of laughter and love,
and friendship beyond death.
This, the most precious thing I own,
so small an offering
on the great rock altar—
till the shifting sunbeam
shines it like a jewel.
"Well offered," says Pellie, in her oracle voice,
"and—
back in the sunlight and the world—
when the purple, the white, and the red are one,
you will thrive too,
for you have faced death's darkness
and will enter life new."

16

I climb back up the dark tunnels in a dream. Daylight blinds me as I step outside, and the sun's heat is on my skin, drying my clothes and warming my blood. Pellie-oracle said life would start new, and I feel it pulsing through me, strong as dark wine, rich as a feast. My feet are strong and sure on the rocky path; the smell of thyme is clean and sharp under my feet. I don't fear wild animals or guards—I know I am safe.

Mama and Nunu are siesta-dozing in the shade of the hut, Chance at their feet. He thumps his tail but is too hot to bother getting up; Mama and Nunu don't stir. Love warms through me as I look down at their sleeping faces, Mama's more peaceful than it ever was before the house fell; Nunu's worn and tired. She tries not to show that weariness to me, soothing me as if I were still a child when I return from the purple.

Yet I'm not a child—and Nunu, no matter how I feel about her, is not my grandmother. She was bought by our family when she was young, to be fed, clothed, and housed in exchange for her labor.

She's working still, and we give nothing back. I've seen her lift food to her mouth—last, always last, after Mama and I have eaten—only to have Mama snatch it for herself. And yet Nunu is the one earning food from the fishers. She doesn't need us.

My heart twists as she stirs and wakes.

"Nunu . . ." I can hardly get the words out. "Do you want to stay here?"

She snorts, gesturing to the ruin-rock hut with its roof of branches. "It's not as if we have choices."

"But you do, Nunu. I can't ask you to stay. You've looked after Mama and me our whole lives, and we can't even feed you now."

I'm not saying this very well. Her face is incredulous, then ferocious.

"Goddess leaping, girl! Who will look after your mother if you throw me out?"

"I'm not throwing you out, Nunu! But you can choose—if you want to live with the fishers, or try to find the craft-folk from home . . . or stay with us. You're free."

"Don't be ridiculous. Free! You and your mama are my family. Am I a kicked dog, to desert you now?"

I feel as deflated as a wrung-out sponge.

"Do you think I can call myself free?" she demands— and despite all the humphing and snorting, her eyes glint with unshed tears—"when my Swallow Clan granddaughter is living as a slave?"

Granddaughter.

Nunu calls me child, calls me by name—calls me frog with the sense of a fish—but she has never been free to call me granddaughter.

"Thank you, Grandmother," I say, and salute her.

I can't explain, to Mama and Nunu or myself, why I won't go to the fishers' midsummer celebration that night. I'm still wearing my ceremonial skirt, and Nunu's afraid that means I'll go to the town feast instead and try to mingle with the priest-folk there.

"I know it's where you belong," she says. "But not now."

"By the great mother's breath," I swear, "I don't want to join the priest-folk. I'll celebrate the goddess alone, as I did this morning at the peak."

Nunu studies me for a long moment, then takes my head in her hands and kisses my forehead. "They may have tricked you into being a purple slave, but there's more of the goddess in you than in all the priests here."

I don't remind her that she hasn't met any priest-folk here. I am too close to tears. And when Mama imitates her, kissing my forehead and each cheek, crooning, "Leilei, Leilei," the tears spill.

"You'll be here when we return?" Nunu asks as they leave for the fishers' beach at sunset.

"Till dawn. I need to be back for the headcount."

Her face clouds. "By the look of you—I hoped that the goddess had answered your prayer and you wouldn't have to return to that foul pit of a place."

"I hoped so too," I admit. "But for now, I have to."

Standing in line for the headcount, the last traces of joy evaporate. I'm trying not to choke as I look over the pots of murex still to be smashed, the heaps of empty broken shells, the pots of rotting purple slime stewing for three days and the tripods waiting to cook the ripest . . .

Pignose looks at me and smirks. "Over here, Not-A-Priestess! You think you're too good for the purple stink?"

"No," I say, trying not to breathe. One day away and the stench is even more sickening than usual.

"You want to get away from it?"

My heart leaps. It can't be true—a new life starting with kindness from Pignose?

He sees my instant of hope and starts to laugh. He laughs till he chokes, because these fumes are stronger even than him. Wheezing, he points to a rough sledge heaped with empty shells. "Take those to the potters."

I've seen men hauling these sledges—never a girl or woman. The men grunt and strain as if they're about to collapse.

He thinks I can't do it—he's still punishing me for being who I am. He follows me as I put the rope around my forehead and lean into it, because he thinks I'll collapse; maybe even die.

He could be right. I'm not sure I'm going to be able to shift it at all.

Of course I can—another tug, and it's moving!
The goddess's joy may be gone, but I can still feel her strength. Whatever the Pellie-oracle meant, it wasn't dying in a sledge harness.

Are you sure?

The further I go the less sure I am. Oracles are tricky—after all, Pellie's mother, when she became the Lady, thought the oracle meant that the time of death was over and our home was safe. I'd be dead too if Dada hadn't read it differently.

This is the hardest work I've ever done. The rope is cutting my forehead, but that doesn't hurt as much as my neck, my back, all the rest of me. I hold the rope with my arms in every different way I can think of; none of them work. My legs are wobbling like jellyfish, but if I fall I'll never get up.

Maybe new life means new life in the underworld.

I'm nearly halfway; I stop to catch my breath at the top of this hill, looking down at the fishers' beach and the road to the town.

My heart is going to thump right out of my chest. Can that happen? It really feels like it could.

Pignose is rushing to catch up now he's seen me pause, waving his stick and shouting unspeakable Pignose insults. I take a deep breath and start down the hill—it's got to be easier than going up.

The sledge goes faster and faster, bumping my wobbly legs, knocking me over—and keeps on going. I roll out of its way just in time. Pignose laughs himself into another coughing fit.

Shells shoot off in every direction as the sledge rocks, nearly tipping over, and shudders to a stop at the edge of the road.

Pignose stops laughing—I think he's disappointed that the sledge didn't tip right over. Or that it didn't run over me. But now he's coughing too hard to follow any further, and has to sit and watch from the top of the hill. If he sees me slow down I'll feel that stick across my shoulders when I return, so I crawl down the hill till my legs can stand, slip the rope across my forehead again, and haul the heavy sledge the rest of the way to the town.

I can't even remember the Leira who believed that a new life would ever be possible.

17

Andras is on guard duty at the gate. He waves me past without looking. I don't want to look at him either. I'm red-faced, dripping with sweat, panting like a dog, wearing a torn shift tied between my knees. And I'm a purple slave. This is not how I want to see the only person here who could have been a friend.

But I don't know where the pottery workshop is, and this sledge is too heavy to haul around town searching for it.

"Where do I take it?"

Andras stares in shock. "Leira? I thought you were going to be a house servant."

"It seems no one wanted to be reminded that priest-folk could fall, and it would be easier if I disappeared."

"I thought you were avoiding me. You weren't even at the sun festival yesterday."

"No." It's too hard to say more, and I'm too exhausted to try. "Where do I take these?"

He points down a lane to the right. "But you'll find it a sad place today. One of the apprentices went to the goddess last night."

Sacrificed? Like the poor slave girl at Tarmara?

"She drank too much ale and fell off the roof where she was sleeping. Her neck broke."

"Not your cousin?"

"No, Teesha is well—no more than a sore head from the feasting, and grief for her friend."

I fix the strap around my forehead again, lean into it, and start hauling. I hope the potter still wants these shells. What will I do if they're all away mourning that poor girl?

It's strange—a year ago I wouldn't have thought anything of this girl, unless she made a pot I wanted. Yesterday I'd have envied her being a potter's apprentice, one of the craft-folk, almost free. Today I feel sorry for her, because although I'm still a purple slave, I'm alive.

The sledge's right runner catches between two stones, spilling shells across the lane. I shove it out, pick up the shells, and catch my breath. A thought is tickling at my mind but I'm too exhausted to hear it. I keep on going.

The workshop floor in front of the storeroom is quiet, but the potter is at her wheel, a boy is stoking the fire at the kiln, and a girl my age with a tear-stained face is preparing clay from the two piles behind her: one of red clay dust and one of white.

When the purple, the red, and the white are one . . .

I have one chance. I don't care if purple slaves aren't supposed to speak, I've got to say all I can; show what I know.

"I've brought the shells to strengthen the clay," I tell the potter. Teesha looks up with a sad half-smile, so I continue. "Is the kiln ready to burn them, so they can be crushed and mixed in?"

"What do you know of mixing clay?" the potter asks.

The lie comes easily, straight from the goddess and Nunu. "My family were potters. Our home and village were lost in the flood, the night of the war of the gods."

"What was your village?"

"No one here has heard of it. It was called Swallow Town, a small settlement outside Tarmara. Everyone has gone."

"So how did you end up at the purple works?"

"I fled here with my mother and grandmother. My mother's spirit left when our house fell on her— she doesn't remember the skills she had, and my grandmother's hands are too old. I was told you had no need of another apprentice so I offered myself as a servant to the palace. But that was the time when the purple needed more workers, so I was sent there."

"Wait here," says the potter, lifting the finished bowl off the wheel. She wipes her hands on her leather potter's kilt, and strides down the lane.

I squat gratefully in the storeroom's shade; the working floor is soft and smooth with years of clay dust. Below us the town stretches toward the harbor where the sailors and fishers are rebuilding their homes and boats. In the months I've been at the purple works, I haven't realized how the wind and occasional shower have washed so much of the ash away; when I look out from here, there are colors everywhere. Behind us the smooth walls of the palace are painted in whites and bright colors, but the rock walls of the buildings around me are golden in the sun. Out to the west the hills are covered in shades of green, from dark to bright to the softest gray-green or gold, with patches of red where clay has been dug, though between the town and the deep blue of the sea are the white hills where we've built our hut in the ruins of the Old Ones.

When the purple, the red, and the white are one . . . I think again. No, it's not just thinking, I'm praying. *Purple* doesn't mean the color, but the leftover shells—when the dye-sac has been stewed into rich, stinking dye, and the rest of the creature eaten, the shells serve one final purpose, strengthening clay so it's less likely to break in the kiln.

Teesha wipes the tears off her face with the back of her hand, smearing red clay and snot across her cheeks. "Are your family really potters?" she asks.

I hesitate. "My grandmother's family," I say at last, because claiming Nunu as a grandmother doesn't seem a lie at all anymore. "I'd only just made my first pot— the first one to be fired—before our home was lost."

"A fired pot already!" she exclaims. "I'm allowed to watch and practice when I finish my work, but I've been mostly hauling dirt and mixing clay for a year now. I've never made anything good enough to fire."

I think of the ugly little jug, so kindly given when we needed it. Then I remember my little saffron pot, the best I'd made—it might have been better than the other girls', but not a pot to be sold or traded. Not a pot to be fired if I hadn't been Swallow Clan.

"It might have been to please my grandmother," I whisper.

Teesha laughs, then lowers her voice too. "Better to tell her that truth than claim more than you are and fail. Her name is Mirna. She's strict but fair."

I trust Pellie-oracle. I even think I'm calm. I think the tightness in my chest is from the strain of pulling the heavy sledge. But when I see Mirna in the laneway I can't breathe.

"It's done," she says simply. "There are any number of poor creatures who can labor in the purple works. There are no others with the beginning of an understanding of clay. You've been reassigned to me. I don't care what you've already learned somewhere else; you will start at the beginning, so don't think your sledge-hauling days are over."

Teesha flashes me a grin, which Mirna sees.

"So Teesha has told you of the joys of getting the raw clay?"

I nod. My throat might as well have a lump of clay stuck in it already, for all the words it can get out.

"But has she told you that if you work well, you'll progress until you're an artisan yourself, free to work wherever you will?"

I still can't speak, but she accepts the nod.

"You'll live here till then, with the family," and she points to the house next to the storeroom.

The sudden bright hope fizzles out like a hot coal in a puddle.

"But my mother and . . .

"Yes, of course," Mirna says impatiently. "Your mother and grandmother too. Goddess forgive me, I have argued rations for them as well, saying they'll be working. No, don't cry, that's the whole point: I don't want an apprentice dripping salt tears into the clay."

18

A full moon goes by;
    the new one brings my bleeding again—
    though I still don't know
    if I can ever be a true woman
    now the Swallow Clan's Learning is gone.
But for now I'm content to learn the clay;
    the digging is heavy,
    the hauling is worse,
    but when it's mixed and ready
    the clay holds magic,
    a smoothness full of unborn pots
    waiting for their potter—
    and one day,
    that will be me.
I could almost sleep
    with the rhythm of rolling
    long ropes of clay for Teesha to wind
    up from the base of a giant pot;
    I roll small balls between my palms

as we did for our saffron bowls—
my thumb in the middle making the hole,
fingers working to smooth the walls—
and though they're only dried in air
not fired in the kiln,
I have made a cup and bowl each
for Mama, Nunu and me,
and a jug as ugly as Teesha's—
jugs aren't so easy.
But Mirna, daughter of potters
since the beginning of time,
sings with her wheel;
pots flow into their forms
between her long-fingered hands,
walls eggshell-thin:
bowls, vases, and cups
all fit to be fired, painted, and sold—
while I, when work is done,
try to mold small bits
as a child might play—
a child like I used to be.
I've made tablets for the palace scribes,
and when Mirna found I could write
I marked tablets for her
with how many feast cups or pots—
or even tablets—
we've supplied to the palace.
Mirna knows who we are
but the palace finds us an uncomfortable truth—
priest-folk who are no longer noble,
from an island that died.

Safest to keep the story
of the lost village near Tarmara
where folk speak with our accent—
because the way I say some words:
"octopus" and "evening" especially,
always sets people laughing—
and we smile when they say "valley"
because they say it like "bottom".
I wear my potter's hide kilt
over my shift, which used to be white,
stained now with purple and red.
My flounced skirt stored
till the day that Dada returns—
and even in my practice pots,
kneaded back into clay again,
I sign a swallow over a crocus,
the seal that would have been mine—
and Andras says
when we are free artisans
he will make me a seal of stone.
Dada will see that mark on a pot,
will wonder and search,
until he finds us.
But what I don't know, when Dada comes,
is whether I want to be priest-folk again
now the land our clan cared for is gone—
because if I wasn't working,
busy all day, tired at night,
grief would swallow me whole.
I know now why Nunu laughed
when I wished my family

could be potters like hers.
I would offer anything
to change life back to how it used to be,
but even the gods can't bring back the dead.
And Pellie, I think, has gone
to the deep underworld
from where there's no return;
she doesn't speak to me now,
in her own or her oracle voice;
my heart calls for her, and aches,
and sometimes, when I laugh with Teesha
or share a look that needs no words,
it aches even more.
So I tell Pellie my life, just in case she can hear,
tell her that Mama has learned to sweep—
she hums and smiles and loves her broom
and Mirna says the workshop floor
is cleaner than it's ever been.
I tell her that Nunu
soothes crying babies
for the mothers in our lane
and is called Grandmother by all.
That Chance has grown tall
and found dog friends to roam with
but always returns
to our feet at night.
That Teesha is clever as well as kind,
sharing friendship,
teaching me more than clay,
and I am teaching her to write.

But the first time
the purple slaves came
with their sledge of shells
my stomach clenched
and I could hardly breathe—
not from the stench
but the memory of fear,
and grief that I've found freedom
while others have not.
I tell her I've learned
to hide the nausea,
smile and thank them—
so Teesha has started to do the same.
And one day,
a master craftsman,
I'll find the small bait-gatherers
to free them into
apprenticeship too.
Then I tell Pellie
of the swallow's nest over
the door of our home;
I've seen swallows dance in the sky
and hope to see fledglings
in the nest come spring.
I tell her that although in our old life
Andras could not be my friend,
he is a true one,
and also:
his voice is deep as a song
his eyes are soft
and he makes me laugh.

19

Autumn comes,
    a full year's circle since the day—
    the start of my Learning journey—
    when the goddess belched
    as we picked her flowers
    and we danced like swallows at sunset
    offering our saffron and ourselves.
The festival here
    is for folk of all clans
    to honor all types of harvest—
    and though it is sparse
    we're the more grateful
    for each grape and grain.
Teesha and I have made cup after cup—
    six hundred and fifty-six
    I marked on the tablet—
    though we made many more
    before Mirna passed them,

because these cups, used once and smashed,
dried but not fired,
still need to be perfect
in the great mother's honor.
But there is no work today—
the wheel is quiet, the kiln cold,
the hundreds of cups stacked in the palace,
waiting for the feast—
but now that my busy hands are still
all that I've tried not to think of
swamps me like the great wave itself.
For this day, when I should become
a woman of our clan
ready to serve the goddess and our land,
there is no one left to teach me
or for me to serve.
This is not something to share with Teesha
so on this strange morning of rest
I walk into the hills
away from the sea and the purple—
to tell Pellie my grief.
"Tonight," I tell her,
  "the Lady and her clan
  will chant the story of their home,
  remembering their folk
  from the beginning of time—
  all those who have died
  but live on in their song.
"But no hymn will be sung
  for the land of the swallows

and it will be lost as if it never was,
as if its folk never lived at all;
as if you had never laughed with me
and swallows had never come to land—
because only a woman grown
can know that song and sing it."
And my dead sister-friend,
silent for three moons,
comes to me at last.
"There are many gifts that please the mother;
there are many rites that make a woman.
As the first woman
once sang the first story,
in this new land you must make your own.
Our land and Learning are gone
but will never die
if you give them life."
So I sing for Pellie,
I sing for my land and all that I've lost,
the stories I know
of our swallow-blessed isle,
of Kora our Maiden,
her belching mother,
and the clans who served them,
from priest to purple.
I sing them all, best as I can
and though my voice breaks,
I sing what no one has told before:
of its terrible death
that it will not be lost.

In reply, the goddess guides me to a rock crevice. Green spikes poke through the ash—and there are the six purple petals of the great mother's flower.

Picking it makes me weep harder than singing the land's death.

I've brought my basket, hoping for mushrooms or berries, but this is better than food. I climb higher, rock to rock and crocus to crocus till when the sun is high, my basket is full of flowers and my heart emptied of tears.

Mama and Nunu greet me as if I'm carrying gold.

"Leilei!" Mama praises, helping me pluck orange threads—she remembers more than we know—and with Mirna's permission, we lay them in the kiln with the smallest fire to dry them.

All afternoon, we listen to the chanting and beating of drums from the palace courtyard as the Lady and her priest-folk prepare for the sacrifices—but we stay home. "To watch the saffron," I tell Teesha, which is partly true.

The other truth is that Mama's face twisted when the chanting started, and Nunu's eyes filled with tears.

It's not enough to sing our land's story alone on the hills—it has to be shared to make it live. To Mama and Nunu now, Dada and Ibi when we find them, anyone from our land that we meet. . .and one day, to my own children and theirs.

The song isn't perfect. I can tell my mistakes by the way Mama blinks in surprise—but they're both weeping as I sing the new ending.

"You've earned your Learning, child," says Nunu, and Mama kisses my forehead. "Don't look so surprised; of course I don't know the Swallow Clan rites you would have done this day, but I've heard the saga often enough to know it."

"But that's not the end of the Learning."

"Do you think anyone ever finishes learning?" demands the only grandmother I've ever known. "But if the great mother has any sense at all, she'll know you've done more Learning this year than any woman has been asked before."

My head is still swimming with this when Teesha runs back, breathless with excitement. "Come on! It's the maidens' procession!"

Just for an instant her voice blurs with Pellie's in my mind. I say yes, though I'm not sure what she means.

The sun is setting, the sky red as the blood of the sacrificed goats, with the swallows dark against it, wheeling in their departure dance.

I stand in the courtyard with Teesha and the other maidens of all the different clans, in my brushed-clean potter's kilt and my once-white shift, splashed with purple and now with the red of clay. A garland of crocus is around my neck, with more in my basket; in my other hand is my own small pot to place on the altar.

I'm the only one with saffron to offer, but every girl here has a basket for the procession. I thank Pellie, thank my Learning, for leading me out to the hills this morning to find what I need for this new rite, as well as the gift for my own goddess.

The road through the town, looping around the houses and craft quarter and back to the palace, is made

272

of broad stones. Today, with the street swept clean, I realize that every third stone has an offering hollow.

Singing, twirling, we dance down the road, out from the palace toward the watch-hill, where Teesha and I met Andras once to see the sun rise between the hills. We take turns marking each offering spot with something from our baskets—tiny seashells, flowers, strands of seaweed—Teesha has made round clay beads, and I have my crocus petals, and though some of the offerings are the same, we each arrange them in a different pattern around the hollow. It seems strange that we don't place our offering inside it, but I watch the others and do what they do.

The youths' procession follows, close enough that they watch us arranging our offerings. They are carrying pitchers of olive oil and flaring torches, and at each spot one of them dribbles oil into the hollow and lights it. Sometimes there's a bit of jostling and shoving to reach one spot first, even though there are so many to choose from. Our whirling dance lets us see them without seeming to watch. Teesha's song is suddenly louder and her dance wilder, and I see that the tall stonemason apprentice is lighting the hollow surrounded by her beads. Mine is the next one—and Teesha's poking me, laughing, as Andras lights it. We link arms and whirl until it's our turn again.

We dance all the way back to the palace courtyard, where the rest of the town is waiting, clapping and chanting, for the feast to begin. Mama and Nunu are there with Mirna and her family, and though I don't know if this is home, for the moment I'm happy.

We dance and eat, laugh and dance, maidens in the middle and the youths stamping, leaping and clapping, stars above us and the lights of the offering lamps circling the town below.

Dancing our grief
for Maiden Kora gone
we honor the great mother's tears
that come as winter rain;
dancing our mourning
till it turns to joy,
and in the midst
of the swirling dancers,
the chanting and clapping,
I dance for the swallows
as we did at home,
wishing them strong flights
to wherever they go,
"But at winter's end," I dance, I beg,
"return with the Maiden,
bring us the spring,
and the wandering travelers
from across the sea."
And the swallows,
roosting in great flocks
before they leave
murmur in reply,
promising that like the Maiden,
life will return.

ACKNOWLEGMENTS

At the very beginning of researching this book, I joined Aegeanet, a group of archeologists and academics who are amazingly willing to answer questions from passionate amateurs of the Aegean Bronze Age. I particularly want to thank Dr. Sabine Beckmann, who became a friend as well as mentor, archeology tutor and experimenter, even making her own murex purple dye for me, and helping me create Leira's name from her theories on Minoan language. The day I spent with her in and around Gournia was a highlight of my life—Leira had to become a potter once I had held a stone pottery tool, stood on the powdery clay floor of the ancient workshop, and seen a piece of pot marked with a 4000-year-old thumbprint . . . Thanks also to the Gournia archeological site, and the staff of INSTAP for their warm welcome and enthusiasm when Sabine explained that I was researching a novel. Any errors in the background facts are purely mine—especially the deliberate ones such as relocating the Psychros Cave to a hill near Gournia.

I also want to mention Katie, our extremely knowledgeable guide to Akrotiri, who I finally coaxed into giving me a personal opinion on the age of the snub-nosed saffron gatherer, not presently on display—and all the archeologists doing this painstaking work and sharing their research with the public.

That trip, and the following twenty-two months

of writing, were made possible by the generosity of the Australia Council, for which I am eternally grateful.

Mark and Kiniki Stirling, who were working with refugees in Greece at the time, gave me a more personal insight into the shock of dislocation. Mirna, of Scheria Greek Art, sent me a totally unexpected gift of her recreation of the dancing swallows fresco from Akrotiri, and inspired the title of the book. And more friends than I can name have supported me with specific areas of knowledge, as well love and enthusiasm.

On the writing side, I am grateful, as always, to the team at Allen and Unwin: Jodie Webster and Kate Whitfield, and Sue Flockhart, who supported the book's gestation and couldn't stop being involved after retiring. It was also wonderful having the involvement of Pajama Press, with Erin Alladin and Gail Winskill. A special thanks to Josh Durham for another brilliant cover, and Sarfaraaz Alladin for equally brilliant maps.

Finally, my family: my husband Tom, as well as the usual support during the vagueness and exhaustion of writing, climbed with me up Mount Juktas and down the Psychros Cave, stayed in the earthquake simulator when I had to escape, and generally made a strenuous trip easy. And because my life is completely interwoven with my writing, I have to thank James and Georgia, Susan and Glyn, for the greatest gifts of all—ten days apart as I finished the first draft. Welcoming Claudia and Olive to the world made me more determined than ever that Leira would grow to womanhood strong and confident in her body, despite the traumas that she faced. May all children do the same.

ABOUT THE AUTHOR

Wendy Orr was born in Edmonton, Canada, but grew up in various places across Canada, France, the US, and the UK before moving to Australia at twenty-one. She started writing when her children were young and eventually gave up her career as an occupational therapist to become a full-time writer. She's the author of many books, including *Nim's Island* (which inspired the feature film), *Raven's Mountain*, *Peeling the Onion*, and *Dragonfly Song*; major awards include the CBCA Book of the Year, the Adelaide Festival Award for Children's Literature, and the Prime Minister's Award for Children's Literature.

Wendy has always been fascinated by ancient history, and one of the greatest adventures of her life was visiting the sites of Crete and Santorini where *Dragonfly Song* and *Swallow's Dance* take place. Under an archeologist's guidance, she handled stone pottery tools, identified shards of Minoan pottery, and stood on the powdery clay floor of the potter's workshop. She descended into the deep, mysterious cave known as the birthplace of the god Zeus, and climbed to the top of a mountain where a Minoan shrine once stood. On the path to the shrine, she found a tiny, smooth white pebble that didn't seem to belong with the rocks around. "It was an offering to the goddess," the archeologist told her. That's why Wendy believes that there's always an element of magic in writing.